THE TIBETAN CORPSE STORIES

THE TIBETAN CORPSE STORIES

by Ācārya Nāgārjuna and King Gautamiputra

Translated by

RYOSHUN KAJIHAMA, Ph.D.

MOTILAL BANARSIDASS PUBLISHERS
PRIVATE LIMITED • DELHI

First Edition : Delhi, 2014

Drawings by Tseten
Stories edited by Alan Neill

ISBN : 978-81-208-3631-0

MOTILAL BANARSIDASS
41 U.A. Bungalow Road, Jawahar Nagar, Delhi 110007
8 Mahalaxmi Chamber, 22 Bhulabhai Desai Road, Mumbai 400026
203 Royapettah High Road, Mylapore, Chennai 600004
236, 9th Main III Block, Jayanagar, Bengaluru 560011
Sanas Plaza, 1302 Baji Rao Road, Pune 411002
8 Camac Street, Kolkata 700017
Ashok Rajpath, Patna 800004
Chowk, Varanasi 221001

Printed in India

by RP Jain at NAB Printing Unit,
A-44, Naraina Industrial Area, Phase-I, New Delhi-110028
and published by JP Jain for Motilal Banarsidass Publishers (P) Ltd,
41 U.A. Bungalow Road, Jawahar Nagar, Delhi-110007

For my wife,
Hiromi Kajihama
with love

Contents

	Preface	ix
	Introductory Story	1
1.	The Rich Man's Son	7
2.	The King and the Minister	13
3.	Pearl Vomiter	21
4.	The Wise Rabbit and the Lion	27
5.	King Paṭapūli	31
6.	Śūnyatā Singh	37
7.	The Horse Keeper Who Never Lied	43
8.	The Partridge Who Avenged Her Chicks' Death	49
9.	The Cattle Herder Who Became a King	53
10.	Lakṣasūrya and Her Previous Lives	61
11.	The Girl Who Retrieved the King's Spirit from Death	67
12.	The Wise King and the Three Sisters	77
13.	The Mother and Daughter Who Tamed the Man-Eating Tiger	85
14.	Masang Yarukhata, the Brave Minotaur	89
15.	The Diviner With the Pig-Head	97
16.	Two Brothers, Sūryaprabha and Candraprabha	107
17.	The Clever Man and the King	115
18.	The Bird-Skin King	119
19.	Painter Ānanda and Carpenter Ānanda	125

20.	The Girl Who Retrieved a Lost Heart	131
21.	The Couple	137
22.	Lady Hemapradīp	141
23.	The Clever Man	149
24.	The Brahman's Son	153
25.	The Trader Who Became a King	161
26.	The Sword of Vajrapāṇi	169
27.	The Wise Minister	175
28.	Lady Kaphalikālaghu	185
29.	The Kind Horse	197
30.	The Girl Who Exchanged Pleasure for Pain	207
31.	The Kingdom Founded on a Trade Route	217
32.	The Fortunate Man	225
33.	A Brother and a Sister	233
34.	The Unmarried Weaver	243

Preface

In the center of Asia and the southwest part of China lies the Tibetan plateau, which is about 4,500 metres above sea level. Given its high altitude, this area is popularly known as the Roof of the World. It is also the source of the major rivers of Asia, these are the Indus, the Salween, the Mekong, the Yangtze, and the Huang Ho River.

In the past, on the plateau there was a country called Tibet and it was divided into three provinces, Ü-Tsang in the west and Kham and Amdo in the east. The people who lived there were called Tibetan. They were introduced to Indian culture as early as the year 600 CE and Indian Buddhism played a major influence. These people established their own individual Tibetan Buddhism which later spread to Mongolia and to other Himalayan regions.

Most of the early Tibetan literature was derived from ancient Indian Buddhist literature. However, one popular non-Buddhist literature that came from India was Vetāla (Vetālapañcaviṁśatikā) or corpse stories. In Tibet it is called, Ro sgruṅ (pronounced Ro Dun) also called, Siddhivad corpse stories, it means stories told by a dead body. It is not clear how or when the Indian Vetāla (corpse stories) came to Tibet, it is presumed they came when Buddhism was introduced into Tibet. Tibetans memorized the corpse stories and transmitted them orally to all parts of Tibet. During that time, the Indian Vetāla (corpse stories) changed into Tibetan stories. They became one of the most important literature in Tibet. Many years later, after the stories had traveled to all of the areas in Tibet, hand-written manuscripts (U Med) were made of them. This is why there are a few different versions of the same stories, because people in different areas remembered them differently.

This book I have translated into English was originally called, *Rgyal bas lung bstan klu sgrub dang rgyal po bde spyod bzang po gnyis kyis mdzad pa'i ngo mtshar rmad du byung ba mi ro gser sgrung.* In English, it could be called, *Fascinating Stories of the Golden Corpse* by Acharya Nāgārjuna and King Gautamiputra. There is no clear information regarding the date and place of its origin, however given the Khampa dialects are scattered throughout the book, we can presume that these stories were influenced by the people and customs of Kham in the eastern part of Tibet. I have collected enough material about the Tibetan Siddhivad corpse stories over the years and I feel they are some of the oldest stories.

As a translator, I did not want to make any mistakes when I translated the old original Tibetan text into English. Since it has many unused Buddhist related words, I had doubts about many of the old Tibetan words. I translated each sentence into English and then asked many Tibetan scholars living in India for help about the difficult terms.

Hundreds of years ago, when the Indian Vetāla stories were first translated from Sanskrit into Tibetan, the names of people and places were changed into Tibetan names and places. I tried to use the original Indian Sanskrit names and places as best as I could. Whenever I encountered difficulty in tracing the original Sanskrit names and places, I used the Tibetan names phonetically.

I want to thank Mr. Tseten for his wonderful drawings in this book, they help reconstruct the wonder I get from these stories. I also want to thank Mr. Alan Neill for editing the stories. I am honored to have my book published by Motilal Banarsidass, one of the renowned publishers in India.

December 2013 Ryoshun Kajihama

Homage to Ācārya Nāgārjuna

Oh Nāgārjuna[1] prophesied by the Victorious One[2] to appear in this world,

You illuminated both outside world and inner inhabitants[3]

By revealing the definitions of the Mādhyamika philosophy.[4]

To the Second Buddha,[5] I humbly pay homage.

Merit of this book

With great sincerity, it strives to understand fully the essence of the fascinating work of Nāgārjuna and King Gautamiputra,[6] which scholars and people believe to be authentic. Merely telling or listening to the stories can fetch both common and uncommon blessings.

1. Nāgārjuna, (Tib. Klu sgrub, Pron. Ludrub) lived in South India circa 150-250 CE. His main works include Mādhyamikakārikā, the seminal work expounding the theory of śūnyatā (emptiness) and the Mādhyamika philosophy. In the later part of his life, Nāgārjuna was held to have converted the author King Gautamiputra of Sātvāhana dynasty to Buddhism.
2. Tib. Rgyal ba, literally meaning victorious one or victor, is an epithet of Buddha Śākyamuni who lived around 560-486 BCE.

3. According to Buddhism, the world is explained in its two-fold aspects: inner and outer, which means the universe and living beings respectively.

4. Mādhyamika, or the Middle Way philosophy established by Nāgārjuna.

5. Second Buddha refers to Acharya Nāgārjuna, who is considered second in the line of importance after Buddha.

6. Tib. Bde spyod bzang po, a possible Tibetan rendition of Sanskrit names Kṣamakarabhadra, Sankarabhadra, or Kandarpabhadra, points to various kings of the Sātvāhana dynasty. It is not clear which one was a disciple of Nāgārjuna. Scholars suggest that this person could be the last king of the Sātvāhana dynasty. Therefore, I preferred to use this name, Gautamiputra. As a young prince, he was assigned by Nāgārjuna to bring a spirit in a corpse named Siddhivad from the Shitavana cemetery. In the process, the corpse tells many stories, which in time became highly popular. These stories told by the corpse were later put into letters and attributed to Prince Gautamiputra and Acharya Nāgārjuna.

Introductory Story

Once upon a time, there lived seven magician brothers in a kingdom in central India. Not far away from them, probably about one Yojana[1] away, there lived two young princes.

One day, the elder prince went to the seven magician brothers' house to learn the secrets of magic. He trained for seven years, but did not learn any magic tricks because the magician brothers withheld their secrets and did not impart them to the elder prince.

One time, the younger prince arrived at the magicians' place to deliver some food to his elder brother. He looked through the door and saw the secrets of their magic, which he spontaneously understood. Instead of handing over the provisions to his brother, the younger prince called him to come out and they returned to their palace. The younger prince said to his elder brother, "Even if you were trained in magic for seven years, you can't be sure that you can know how to do it. In our own compound, there is a really wonderful horse. Take it, but do not let it go towards the seven magicians' house. Head in the opposite direction and sell the horse, buy things and bring them here." Having said this, the younger prince changed himself into a magic horse.

The elder prince thought that, although I learned magic for seven years, I could not be perfect in it. My younger brother perfected such a wonderful skill. What would happen if I rode the horse? As soon as he mounted the horse, a force of magic turned the horse and the horse traveled towards the seven magicians' house. When they arrived at the gate, there was no way the younger prince could escape. Thinking that the seven magician brothers might be interested in buying the horse, the elder prince said to them, "This is a wonderful horse found by my younger brother, would you like to buy it?" They knew it was a magic horse and they were afraid that the younger prince might know all about their magic secrets. So, they decided to buy and kill the horse. The magician brothers paid as much as the elder prince demanded for it. Then the seven magician brothers tied the horse to a fence.

Later, some brothers held the horse by the ears, while others held it by the legs and the tail so that it could not escape. They took the horse to a river, they wanted to give the horse water to make sure the horse bled heavily. The younger prince, who had changed into that horse, knew that his brother had made a mistake that put him in a lot of danger. He wondered which animal form he must change into. Just then, the horse saw a fish in the river and he changed himself into a fish. The seven brothers turned into seven swans and chased the fish. Finding it hard to escape, he changed into a pigeon and flew high in the sky. The seven brothers at once turned into seven hawks and chased him over mountains and into valleys. The pigeon fled into a cave called Śaṃkara[2] in Śrīparvata[3] Mountain in the southern Vaidarbha[4] kingdom and sat in the lap of Acharya Nāgārjuna.

The seven hawks approached near the cave and then they changed into seven dancers. Acharya Nāgārjuna wondered why a pigeon was chased by seven hawks. He asked the pigeon, "Why are you so frightened?" The pigeon told everything that had happened and said, "They are at the entrance of this cave in the form of seven dancers, they will come to you and request that you give a bead from your rosary. I will hide in the form of the knot bead. So, please keep the knot bead in your mouth and scatter the rest of the beads outside." Like he said, the seven dancers came in the cave and requested Acharya Nāgārjuna, "Give us your rosary." Acharya Nāgārjuna kept the knot bead in his mouth and he scattered the rest of his beads outside the cave. The beads at once turned into worms. The dancers turned into seven roosters and right away they all started to eat the worms. Acharya Nāgārjuna took the knot bead out of his mouth and it immediately transformed back into the young prince. The prince took a stick

and killed all the seven roosters and then they turned back into seven human dead bodies.

Acharya Nāgārjuna was extremely displeased and said, "I saved your life, but it resulted in the death of seven men, which is not good." The younger prince said, "I am a prince, Acharya Nāgārjuna has saved my life, but the seven brothers have died. To purify this sin and to repay your kindness, I am ready to obey whatever you ask me to do." Nāgārjuna said, "In a cemetery called Śītavana,[5] there is a corpse called Siddhivad,[6] whose lower body is made of gold, and its upper body is made of turquoise. The hair on its head looks like a conch shell. Can you bring it to me? If you could, all my wishes will be fulfilled. Also, this act shall give collective blessings to all the people of Jambudvīpa[7] and they will live for a thousand years."

The younger prince agreed and said, "I'll do what you want, please tell me about the route, the method and the supplies I will need to do this." Acharya Nāgārjuna said, "The route is about one Yojana away, passing through a narrow, gloomy and eerie valley filled with huge corpses. When you approach, all the corpses will rise up. Bless the biggest corpse with the words 'Hala, Hala, Svaahaa' and sprinkle barley from this small bag.[8] Next, after crossing one valley, there are many baby corpses. They should be blessed by saying 'Tira, Tira Phat' and throw some grains of barley from this small bag. From among these corpses, the Siddhivad will run away and climb up and sit on a mango tree. Pretend to cut the tree with this ax called, Śuklacandra.[9] The corpse will come down. Tie him with this rope that is called, 'small rope that ties hundreds'[10] and put the Siddhivad in this big sack that is called, 'small sack that holds hundreds'[11] and return here.

You have to walk all day and all night while eating this everlasting butter food and you must not say a single word. Prince, as you have arrived here at the cave Śaṁkara, from now on you shall be called, Prince Gautamiputra."

As instructed, the prince set forth on his mission. The prince faced all the dangers on the way and then finally, saw the corpse called Siddhivad. As he chased the corpse, it climbed up a mango

tree. He went near the root of the tree and boastfully shouted, "My teacher is Nāgārjuna, my ax is Śuklacandra and my food is everlasting butter food. I am Gautamiputra. Either you come down or I will cut down this old tree." The corpse cried, "Please don't cut the tree, I'll come down."

Prince Gautamiputra grabbed the corpse, forced him in the bag, tied it together using a rope and carried it on his back while eating the everlasting butter food. After walking for many days, the Siddhivad corpse said, "The day is long and tiring. So why don't you tell a story?" The prince did not reply. The Siddhivad corpse said, "If you like to tell a story, just nod your head. If you want me to tell a story, raise your head." The prince raised his head.

---

1. Yojana (Tib. Dpag tshad, Skt. Yojana) is a measurement of distance used in India since the early Vedic times. For some, a Yojana is equal to 7-8 kilometres, while for others it is equal to 10-14 kilometres.
2. Tib. Bde byed (Skt. Śaṁkara), meaning an enjoyable act.
3. Tib. Dpal gyi ri (Skt. Śrīparvata), literally meaning glorious mountain, refers to the present-day area of Nagarjunakonda in South India.
4. Tib. Be da ha (Skt. Vaidarbha) is a community in South India extant since the Indian Puranic times.
5. Tib. Bsil ba'i tshal (Skt. Śītavana), meaning the cool cemetery.
6. Tib. Dnos grub can (Skt. Siddhivad), means having special powers.
7. Tib. 'Dzam bu gling (Skt. Jambudvīpa), according to Indian cosmology, refers to the world of the humans.
8. Tib.Thun. A small bag used to carry medicine and munchies.
9. Tib.Zla ba dkar po (Skt. Śuklacandra) literally means white moon.
10. Tib. Brgya khros khra mo.
11. Tib. Brgya shong khra mo.

1 The Rich Man's Son

The Siddhivad corpse narrated the first story:

Long ago, there lived a rich man's son, a carpenter's son, a physician's son, a blacksmith's son, an astrologer's son and a painter's son in a great kingdom. Spoiled by their parents' pampering, they left for another country to search for their fortune.

As they arrived at the lower part of a valley, each one planted a life tree.[1] They promised to meet again after six years at that same place. If anyone failed to return or their life tree had dried up, they agreed to search for the person. Having all agreed to do this, they entered the valley in search of food.

The rich man's son walked towards the upper valley. At the point, where the rich forest ended and a sprawling meadow unfolded, there was a small hut. A very old couple lived there. They asked him, "Boy, where did you come from and where are you going?" He replied, "I have come from a distant kingdom in search of food." The elderly couple said, "It is nice that you have come here. We have a daughter, she is very beautiful to behold. You should marry her and be our son-in-law." As they were discussing this, the girl came outside the hut. The rich man's son thought, "My purpose of leaving my parents and coming to this place has been fulfilled. She is more beautiful than an angel." He decided to marry her and stay there. The girl welcomed him and asked him many questions. They both lived happily at that place.

In the lower part of the same valley was a kingdom ruled by a great king. During the summer, the king's attendants came to swim and play in a nearby river. They found a heavily decorated ring that belonged to the wife of the rich man's son, but it had been lost in the river. Amazed by its beauty, they offered it to the king. The king said, "Well, there should be a lady in the upper valley who used to wear this ring. Go, find her." As they went to the upper valley, they saw the woman and she enchanted them by her beauty. They found her extremely beautiful and told her, "You must come with us to the king's court." They brought her and also the rich man's son to the king. When the king saw her, he found her as beautiful as an angel and comparing her beauty to his other queens, he found them to be like pigs and dogs. The king loved her very much, but she only felt love for the rich man's son. The king summoned his servants and commanded, "Kill the rich man's son." As the king ordered, the servants took him to a nearby river. They dug a pit and killed him by crushing him under a huge rock.

Then sometime later, when the six friends were to have their sixth year meeting, only five of the friends came back to the place where they planted their life trees. All were present except the rich man's son. They also saw his life tree had dried up. They were worried and went into the valley to search for him, but they searched in vain and could not find him. The astrologer's son calculated and said, "The rich man's son is dead under a big rock near a river bank." They went there, but they were helpless, as they could not move the rock. The blacksmith's son took out his hammer and split the rock into pieces, dug the ground and removed the dead body. The physician's son prepared a resuscitating potion and put it into the corpse's mouth. The rich man's son came back to life. They asked him, "What caused your death?" He told the whole story to them. They said, "She must indeed be an amazing woman." They all discussed about how to bring the woman back to their friend. The carpenter's son made a mechanized wooden Garuḍa[2] which could carry people up into the air. It could fly by hitting a nail from below to make it go up and hitting the same nail on the top, to make it descend. When it was hit from the side, it could move straight ahead. Finally, the painter's son painted the wooden bird with many different colors.

The rich man's son boarded the flying machine and glided over the roof of the palace. The king and his subjects were surprised to see this strange bird. The king asked the queen, "I have never seen such a bird before. Go to the roof and feed the bird." The queen did what the king asked and she was there when the bird landed on the roof. At the door of the wooden Garuḍa, the rich man's son and the queen met each other. The queen was overjoyed and said, "I thought, I would never see you again. My meeting you was possible due to the miracle of this wooden Garuḍa. How did this happen?" He told her the entire story. Then he said, "Now who do you wish to be? Do you want to remain the queen or do you want to be my life partner forever? If you want to be my wife again, get aboard this wooden Garuḍa. We will fly into the sky and no one can harm us." The queen said, "I love you, a first friend is the best friend." Saying this, she entered the Garuḍa and flew away into the sky. The king and his subjects were shocked and fell down on the ground. They cried out, "We sent the queen to feed the beautiful bird and now she is carried away." The rich man's son in the bird struck the nail down and he landed at the place where his friends were.

First the rich man's son came out and his friends asked, "Was your mission successful?" He replied, "Very successful." Next the queen came out and his friends saw a very beautiful woman. Everyone fell in love with her. Then the rich man's son said, "My friends have helped me, they brought me back to life and also worked to get my wife back. I am grateful to all of you. Now she and I will live together as husband and wife."

The astrologer's son did not agree. He said, "I made the calculations to find where you were lost. So, I should get the queen." The blacksmith's son objected to this and said, "You may have located him with your calculations, but when he was under the rock and helpless, I split the rock with my hammer. The queen should be mine." The physician's son disagreed. He said, "Although you broke the rock, a dead body could not be together with the queen. It was my resuscitating potion that I administered and brought life back to the rich man's son. Thus you were all

able to get the queen back, but I should have the queen." The carpenter's son said, "There was no way we could enter the palace and we could not wage war against the king. I made the wooden Garuḍa to get the queen. Therefore the queen is mine." The painter's son said, "The queen did not come to feed your colorless wooden Garuḍa. I painted it like a Garuḍa and got the queen back. So, I should get the queen." Then everyone said, "Then let us kill her and cut into pieces."

Prince Gautamiputra could not help to say, "Oh, what a pity!" The Siddhivad corpse gleefully said, "The unfortunate prince spoke. Now I shall not stay, I will fly away." Then, the Siddhivad corpse escaped.

Here ends the first Siddhivad corpse story, The Rich Man's Son.

1. Tib. Bla shing, meaning life-tree, are planted to foretell the condition of one's life. The drying of the tree is normally considered a bad omen and indicating an imminent danger to the planter's life.

2. Tib. Bya khyung (Skt. Garuḍa) is a gigantic mythical bird in Indian mythology. The Hindu god Viṣṇu is said to have a Garuḍa as his mount.

2 The King and the Minister

Again, Prince Gautamiputra followed the same route back to Śītavana cemetery. He caught the Siddhivad corpse, forced the corpse into the bag, tied it together using a rope and flung the bag on his back and started to walk.

The Siddhivad corpse then narrated the following story:

Long ago, there was a king, who ruled over a great kingdom. There was a big lake in the upper part of the kingdom. Two Nāga[1] frogs had blocked its outlet and stopped the water supply to the farmers. Every year, all the families in the kingdom took turns to send one person, whether of high or low birth, to go to be the Nāga frog's food.

One day, it was the king's family turn to go. He could not refuse, as it was the law decreed by the king. In the king's royal family, there was only the king and the prince. The king and the prince both decided to go, but they were equally worried. The king said, "I am old, so I should go. My son, you should righteously rule the kingdom." The prince replied, "My godly father, you are ruling the kingdom righteously, therefore you must not go. If you marry again, you will get as many sons as you desire. So, I should go to the frogs." Thus, it was decided that the prince should go and the public sadly came to see him off.

The prince had a childhood friend, who was the son of a minister. The prince went to his friend and said, "Now according to the rule of the kingdom, I must obey the king's order. Therefore, I am going to become the frog's food. You be obedient to your parents and take care of your health." The minister's son became very sad and asked the prince, "Since childhood, I was brought up by your kindness. Please allow me to go instead of

you. Oh prince, I beg you not to go." The prince did not care who went, so they both went there together.

When the prince and minister's son arrived at the edge of the lake, they heard the golden and turquoise frogs having a discussion. One said, "If the prince and the minister's son know our words, they would strike us with a stick on our heads to kill both of us. The prince could then swallow a golden frog and the minister's son could swallow a turquoise frog. Then they will be able to vomit gold and turquoise gems. This would save everybody from coming to us as food in the future, but they are not aware of this." Since the prince knew the language of all the animals, they killed the frogs by striking them on their heads with a stick. They swallowed the frogs and vomited as much gold and turquoise gems as they wished. The minister's son said, "Now that we have killed the frogs and released the water, let us return to our kingdom." The prince refused to do this, saying, "If we return to our kingdom, people may say we are living corpses. Instead, let us go to a better, distant place."

The prince and the minister's son crossed a nearby mountain pass. On reaching the base of the pass, they arrived at a bar that was run by a mother and a daughter. The mother and the daughter offered them wine and asked them to pay for it, they just vomited gold and turquoise gems. After this, the mother and the daughter invited them inside the bar and served them a lot more wine. They got drunk and vomited more gold and turquoise gems and became unconscious. When they regained consciousness, they found themselves outside the bar.

The prince and the minister's son walked towards the lower part of the valley. In the middle of a field, they saw many children fighting among themselves. The minister's son asked, "Why are you fighting?" The children said, "We have found an invisible making hat on the ground and we are unable to agree who should own the hat." He asked, "What is the use of it?" The children said, "Whoever wears this hat becomes invisible to the gods, devils and humans." The minister's son said, "Then let me keep the hat. All of you should race to me from the far end of this field and whoever comes first, will get the hat." The children went to do that, but when they raced back, they did not find the minister's son. The minister's son had put the hat on and he had become invisible. The children said, "He was here a moment ago, but not anymore." They could not find the minister's son and they all returned home crying.

Then the prince and the minister's son walked through a street where they saw many devils arguing. They asked, "What are you arguing about?" The devils replied, "We disagree on who should have these shoes." They asked, "What are they useful for?" "As soon as you put them on, you will reach wherever you wish," replied the devils. The minister's son said, "Why not have all of you race from the end of the street back to me. Whoever comes first, gets the shoes." As the devils raced up, they saw nothing there and yelled, "They were here a moment ago, but now they have disappeared." The devils then went away. Then, slipping into one shoe each and wearing the invisible making hat, they said, "Take us to a kingdom, where they are looking for a king." They prayed and went to sleep. The next morning, the prince and the minister's son found themselves in the hollow of a huge tree in a kingdom that was looking for a new king. That day, there was a big public gathering and the people said, "The person's head that has a ritual cake land on it, thrown by the Conqueror Deity of the Sky,[2] he shall be anointed king." As the deity flung the ritual cake, it fell on the tree where the prince and the minister's son were hiding in it. The crowd shouted, "What does this mean? A tree can't become a king." Then someone said, "Let us see, we never know who could be inside the tree." The people searched and then found the prince and the minister's son inside the hollow trunk. The crowd of people did not believe it and said, "They seem to be foreigners. We will have to do the vomiting competition tomorrow."

The next day, some people drank milk and had white vomit. Some ate vegetables and had green vomit. There were vomit of all types and colors. The prince vomited gold and said, "I'll be the king of this country." The minister's son had blue vomit of turquoise gems and declared, "I will be the minister of the country." Therefore, they became the king and the minister. The beautiful princess of the former king became the queen.

There was a towering fortress near the palace and the queen visited the fortress every day. After some time, the minister's son, who was now a minister, was curious about the queen's regular visits to the fortress. He wondered if there was somebody inside. One day, the minister put on the invisible making hat and followed the queen when she walked to the fortress. The queen opened the doors and climbed all the way up the stairs to the roof. Then she arranged a high comfortable silk seat, took off her dress, washed her body and put on a silk dress. She applied scents and made herself beautiful. She sat down and made offerings of teak[3] incense. The minister with the invisible making hat sat near her. After a short while, a very beautiful bird appeared from the sky. The queen welcomed the bird with incense as it landed on a very smooth slab on the roof. From inside the bird's body came a young god, who was unimaginably handsome. They embraced each other, sat on the silk cushion and enjoyed various food and drinks. The divine son said, "How was your husband selected by the Conqueror Deity of the Sky a few days ago?" The queen replied, "I don't know much about it, but he is a young man and I have not seen a fault in him." They separated by saying, "Let us meet again tomorrow morning." The queen packed everything up and returned to the king.

The next day, the queen walked towards the fortress as usual and the minister followed her with the help of the invisible making hat. That day, the young god said, "I'll come tomorrow to see your husband in the form of a bird." The queen agreed and they parted. The next morning, the minister said to the king, "There is a youthful god in the fort" and then told the whole story. The minister said, "This morning, light a big fire. Catch all the small birds by the tail and throw them into the fire. Also, make sure you kill them all with your sword."

The next morning, as scores of people waited to greet the king, perched on a staircase was the young god in the form of a

colorful bird. The minister put on the invisible making hat and caught the bird by its tail feathers and threw it into a fire. The king advanced to strike the bird with his sword, but the queen caught the king's hand and the blade missed the bird. With only a few burnt feathers, the bird flew into the sky. The queen was terrified and almost fainted.

The next day, the minister again put on the invisible making hat and followed the queen as she walked to the fortress. The queen arranged everything as before and waited, but the young god did not appear. Gazing sadly into the sky, she waited and waited. After some time, the bird appeared. Now he had turned into a leper, full of sores on his body with puss, blood and serum oozing out. The queen held him and wept. The young god said, "Don't cry. Though your husband looked majestic, he threw me into the fire for no reason. As my body endured severe burns, I will not be able to come to see you as frequently as before." Having promised to meet once every month, the divine son soared into the sky. The queen developed more respect and love for the king.

Wearing the invisible making hat, the minister said, "I am leaving this palace." He left and arrived at the gate of a temple. As he looked through the space of a door, he saw the temple caretaker wrapping himself up in a paper roll with a drawing of a donkey on it. He immediately changed into a massive donkey and dashed around to all parts of the temple braying loudly. As he lied down on his back, he returned to the form of the caretaker. Then he stuck the paper roll under the arm of a statue and left the temple. The minister took the paper roll and went to the mother and the daughter who sold them wine who last time badly treated him and his friend. He said, "I have come to repay your kindness." To deceive them, he gave them three gold coins. The mother and daughter wine sellers said, "You are a nice man. How did you get these gold coins?" He replied, "I rolled on this paper roll and got all this gold." They requested, "Let us roll on the paper." As they did, they turned into two donkeys. He took them to the king and said, "Let them carry the mud and stones for the construction of a fort." The donkeys worked for three years, and grew sores on their backs. They cried whenever they saw the king. The king said to the minister, "These donkeys are not well. So don't be cruel to them." The minister let them roll on the paper again and they turned into two frail old women. Their bodies were full of sores with puss and blood on their bodies.

Prince Gautamiputra could not help to say, "Oh, what a pity!" The Siddhivad corpse gleefully said, "The unfortunate prince spoke. Now I shall not stay, I will fly away." Then, the Siddhivad corpse escaped.

Here ends the second Siddhivad corpse story, The King and the Minister.

1. From the three-fold division of universe, heaven, earth and nether world, the Nāgas (Tib. klu) inhabit the realms of the spirit world. They often live in water bodies and assume different forms, mostly of reptiles such as snakes and frogs.
2. Tib. A phyi gnam gyi gung rgyal ma.
3. Tib. Agar (Skt. Akaru), refers to all kinds of tropical hardwood tree of teak genus.

3 Pearl Vomiter

Again, Prince Gautamiputra followed the same route to Śītavana cemetery, and arrived near the tree where the Siddhivad corpse was in. The corpse pleaded, "Please don't cut this old tree, I'll come down." The prince carried the corpse on his back and traveled on. The corpse said, "It is a long journey and we are both tired and bored. Either you tell a story or you can raise your head, if you want me to tell a story." The prince raised his head.

The Siddhivad corpse then narrated the following story:

Once there lived a king, who ruled over a great kingdom. In the upper valley, there was a man named Pearl Vomiter.[1] He lived with his wife and he vomited pearls whenever he was happy.

One day, the king dispatched a messenger to summon him to the court to vomit pearls. His wife said, "Please take me along whenever you go to the king's court or please draw your image on the wall above our bed for keepsake." She then pretended to be very sad. The husband said, "I can't take you with me to the king's court. So, for your sake, I'll draw my image for you." He drew a portrait of himself on the wall near his bed. Then he left for the king's palace and after traveling some distance, he remembered that he had forgotten his rosary that was in his bed. He returned home to fetch his rosary. When he looked through the door of his house, he saw his wife on their bed making love with the neighbor. The neighbor said, "It seems that this portrait on the wall can speak to you." She grabbed a handful of dust and threw it on the portrait, saying, "Let him eat this." When Pearl Vomiter saw this, he became very sad and went to the palace.

The king guided Pearl Vomiter into the palace and served him expensive and splendid food and drinks, the king thought that Pearl Vomiter must now be satisfied. The king asked him, "Now why don't you vomit pearls for me?" Disturbed by the conduct of his wife and his neighbor, Pearl Vomiter was depressed and could not vomit pearls. The king and his ministers discussed ways to make Pearl Vomiter happy. They giggled and laughed and played various stunts to amuse him. To surprise him the king threw a flower to the queen. The queen responded with a frown, as if displeased. Pearl Vomiter was still disturbed emotionally and could not vomit pearls. The king said, "I extended to you an honor given for a priest, served luxurious meals and bestowed to you a lot of gifts. However, you disrespected my order to vomit pearls. You deserve now to be punished." The king ordered the ministers, "Put him in the inner section of the foul smelling pigsty." The ministers did what the king ordered and locked him in the pigsty.

Days later, the pig keeper, who had a cleft lip, brought pigs to put them in the pigsty. He waited at the door holding a heavy stick. Pearl Vomiter watched and wondered why the pig keeper was standing there. After a few hours, Pearl Vomiter saw the queen come in and walk towards the pig keeper. The pig keeper was very angry and beat her three times with the heavy stick, saying, "How long have I been waiting for you." The queen said, "My only lover, please don't be angry. It took longer to lull the king to sleep. I could not come until now. So don't speak like this." She curled herself around his neck, kissed him and put her tongue to his lips. Pearl Vomiter watched this in wonder. Pearl Vomiter thought that maybe it was difficult to trust women. He recalled, "Last time, my wife asked me to draw my portrait for keepsake when I was away. I believed her to be telling me the truth. However, my wife invited the neighbor into my bed and threw dust on my portrait saying, 'Let him eat this!' In a similar manner, the queen seem displeased when the king teased her with a flower. Also, tonight she enjoys fondling and kissing the ugly pig keeper on his cleft lip as if she was licking a mouthwatering dish. Then she was flogged three times by the pig keeper. Both women found other men irresistible and preferred them to their husbands." He wondered how unreliable women are and how fast they change their minds. He was so bewildered at this, that he vomited. As he began to laugh, he vomited so many pearls, he filled up almost half of the pigsty.

When the king heard about the vomit, he summoned Pearl Vomiter to the court and asked him, "Why is it that you did not vomit when served the best food and drinks and bestowed with splendid gifts? Yet you now dare to vomit pearls in that dingy pigsty?" Pearl Vomiter said to the king, "When you summoned me to vomit pearls, my wife asked me to draw my portrait for her. Thinking she really wanted it, I drew my portrait on a wall and left for your court. However halfway there, I returned to fetch my rosary that I left behind. Then I saw my wife making love with our neighbor. While in the bed, I saw her throw a handful of dust on my portrait saying, 'Let him eat this!' After seeing this, I came to your palace, sad and depressed. Even when served with wonderful food and drinks and entertained and amused by amazing stunts, I was emotionally hurt and I could not vomit pearls. The last time, when your highness threw a flower to the queen, she frowned. I saw the queen come to see the cleft lipped pig keeper at the pigsty. The pig keeper flogged her with a heavy stick three times for arriving late. Yet, even then, the queen lovingly said to him, 'My only lover, please don't be angry. It took longer to lull the king to sleep. I could not come until now. So don't speak like this.' She curled herself around his neck, kissed him, put her tongue to his lips and they made love. I thought women are foolish and bad mannered. Completely bewildered, I laughed and vomited a lot of pearls." The king said, "You are right, we both are deceived by our wives."

The king banished the queen and the cleft lipped pig keeper into exile. He asked Perl Vomiter to send his wife and also the neighbor to the remotest of places. The king then said, "We will rule the country together and get a wife who is neither attractive nor sexually immoral." Pearl Vomiter asked the king, "How can we examine whether a woman is sexually immoral and lustful or not?" The king said, "There is a way to examine women. We must first invite all the women in the kingdom and seat them naked on a sheet of paper. Then we will bring many male and female

donkeys and let them mate. The paper will stick only to the bottoms of women who are immoral. The one who does not stick to the paper, shall be our queen."

An old mother and daughter who lived close, overheard this conversation and talked about it. The old woman said, "If all the women under his rule are summoned, we are sure to be invited as well." The daughter said, "I've never been touched by any men before. So if I sit on the paper, it will not stick to my bottom." The old woman said, "It is true that you've not been spoiled by a man. However, overcome by sexual desire, it will not be possible for the paper not to stick. I have a great idea. Apply butter on a piece of cloth and block your lotus-like vagina."

The next day, the king summoned all the women of his kingdom and made them sit naked on paper sheets. Then donkeys were tempted to mate in front of these women. There was only one single woman without paper sticking on her. The old woman's trick worked, the paper did not stick to her daughter's bottom. The king and the man said, "She is suitable to be our queen." They made the old woman's daughter their queen and they ruled the kingdom.

Prince Gautamiputra could not help to say, "Oh, woman can't be trusted." The Siddhivad corpse gleefully said, "The unfortunate prince spoke. Now I shall not stay, I will fly away." Then, the Siddhivad corpse escaped.

Here ends the third Siddhivad corpse story, Pearl Vomiter.

1. Tib. Mu tig skyug (Skt. Amātyamuktachardi), means the one who vomited pearls.

4 The Wise Rabbit and the Lion

Once again, Prince Gautamiputra journeyed back to get the Siddhivad corpse and arrived at Śitavana cemetery. The prince carried the corpse on his back and traveled on. The corpse said, "It is a long and tiresome journey. Listen, I'll tell you a story." Without uttering a single word, the prince raised his head to listen.

The Siddhivad corpse then narrated the following story:

Long ago, a rabbit, a fox and a wolf met on a high mountain pass. They saw a sorcerer, coming from the middle of the valley, sporting a black hat, carrying a backpack and holding an offering tray in his hand. The rabbit said, "Let us take his backpack and everything in it." The fox and wolf said, "We can't get it." Then the rabbit cleverly said, "I have a way to get it. I will go limping in front of him and as he drops his backpack to chase me. You can grab it and carry it away." The rabbit bent his foot and weakly hopped on one foot. The man, hoping for an easy kill, picked up two heavy stones, dropped his pack on the road and chased the rabbit. The rabbit limped very slowly and was very close to the man, but did not let him catch him. Having led the man away some distance, the rabbit hopped faster and faster. The man was very tired and took a rest. The fox and the wolf carried the backpack and the prayer objects and planned to meet the rabbit later, across the pass.

When they opened the pack, it contained a big chunk of butter, a big cube of sweetened cheese,[1] a mat and a small bag of salt, which they were going to share. Keeping aside both the butter and the sweetened cheese, the rabbit said, "These should be enough of a gesture to that man." He left the butter and the cheese as if they were no good. The rabbit then said, "Dear Fox, since your children are growing up, you might need this bag of salt. Dissolve this in water and apply it repeatedly to the body of your children and they will grow rich fine fur. Dear Wolf, you will need this bell. If you ring this bell next to the ears of your children, it will deafen their ears when the sheep fight each other and your children won't be frightened." The fox and the wolf believed the rabbit's words and accepted the salt and the bell. When the fox applied the salty water on their body, all the fur fell off and they looked naked. The wolf rang the bell in the ears of her cubs, their eardrums burst and they were so frightened that they died. The wolf wondered what could have happened to the fox and went to see him. They told their story to each other. They said, "It seems that the rabbit has deceived us, let us go and kill him."

After three days, the rabbit thought, "I have totally enjoyed the tasty butter and the sweetened cheese, but that fox and wolf might come back to take revenge." Three times he dipped himself in water, rolled on sand and soiled his hair, then he lied in his bed baring his teeth with his eyes rolled upward. He pretended to be almost dead. The fox and the wolf came to the rabbit and they said, "You have harmed us greatly. Now we have come to kill you." The rabbit replied, "You both look healthy. For me, my fur is all burnt, my eyes damaged and my lips are split into four parts. That man surely has great magical power." He pretended to be unable to speak anymore and remained in bed. The fox and the wolf said, "The rabbit is not at fault" and they went away.[2]

Because of eating too much butter and sweetened cheese, the rabbit felt thirsty. He climbed down to the base of the mountain and hopped to the big lake on the western side. He drank a lot of water and slept on a raised rock near the shore.

After some time, it started to snow. The snow that had collected on the branches and leaves of the trees fell into the lake with a heavy splash. Fearing something to be coming out of the water, the rabbit sprang up and took to his heels. On the way, the rabbit met the wolf, who asked, "Friend Rabbit, why you are running?" "There was a splash sound in the lake. So I am running," replied the rabbit hurriedly. The wolf mistook the word 'splash' for the name of a wild beast and he ran with the rabbit. Then

they met a tiger on the pass. The tiger asked, "Why are you two running?" The rabbit told the tiger about the splash sound in the lake and the tiger followed them. On their way, they saw a lion majestically shaking his mane, baring his fangs and scratching his claws. The lion asked, "Who are you running from?" The rabbit told the same story, but the lion became furious and roared, "I am the snow lion, the king of beasts. There is no one who can challenge me. You must be lying, for there is none called 'splash' in the lake." The lion grabbed the rabbit, almost killing him. The rabbit immediately pleaded, "Oh, great King of the Beasts, in the lake, I saw the one called 'splash,' nine times more majestic than Your Majesty. If you would come to the lakeshore, you can see it for yourself." "Then let us go. I must see this beast," said the lion.

The rabbit took the lion to the lake and did not know what to do. The rabbit went on the rock where he slept and then looked down into the water. As he saw his own image in the water, he turned to the lion and said, "The monstrous 'splash' is right here. Climb the rock and look down into the water." The lion did this and saw his own reflection in the water. Misconceiving his own reflection for the beast, the lion became restless and shook his turquoise mane. He saw the reflection repeat his moves. Infuriated, the lion jumped into the lake and died.[3]

Thus goes the saying,

> Like a rabbit frightened by the unfounded 'splash',
> Like an arrogant lion who causes his own death.

Prince Gautamiputra could not help to say, "Although the rabbit was physically small, he was mentally wise and brave." The Siddhivad corpse gleefully said, "The unfortunate prince spoke. I shall not stay, I will fly away." Then, the Siddhivad corpse escaped.

Here ends the fourth Siddhivad corpse story, The Wise Rabbit and the Lion.

---

1. A traditional Tibetan sweetmeat made from a mixture of cottage cheese, cream, butter, honey and molasses.
2. Similar story can be seen in the Pañcatantra and the Vinaya.
3. A similar story is found in the Pañcatantra.

5 King Paṭapūli

Once again, Prince Gautamiputra journeyed the same route and carried the Siddhivad corpse from Śītavana cemetery. The corpse said, "The journey is long and tiresome. So, you tell me a story and I'll listen or I'll tell a story and you listen." The prince raised his head and continued to listen.

The Siddhivad corpse then narrated the following story:

Once in a city, there lived a poor couple and their son. One day, as the son was playing, he saw a rabbit under a bush. With both ears folded backward and eyes closed, the rabbit was in a deep sleep. Wanting to kill the rabbit, the boy quietly picked up a stone. As he walked closer to the sleeping rabbit, he felt pity for the rabbit. He threw the stone away and held the rabbit in his lap.

The rabbit asked, "Why did you pick me up?" The boy replied, "I first wanted to kill you, but I couldn't. So I picked you up and put you in my lap." The rabbit said, "It is good that you didn't kill me, for I might be of great help to you in the future. So, let us stay together." The boy and the rabbit decided to stay together. They then walked into a new territory and arrived at a huge red rock on a desolated mountain pass. There was an entrance to a cave and they went inside. There, they saw a multi-storey fortress with beautiful doors and windows. They went inside to see if someone lived in the back. Inside the place, they saw an inexhaustible stock of wealth and delicious food. In one of the rooms, they also saw many ghosts. The rabbit said, "We have arrived at a very strange place. Let us leave early tomorrow morning. Behind us, at the end of this mountain pass, a king is going to perform an exorcism. Let us go there and watch. We will be able to eat a lot of ritual cake[1] and baked grains too. There will be wonderful things to see."

The ghosts overheard the conversation and wanted to also see this. Therefore, they followed the boy and the rabbit. The royal priests played drums and pipes to perform the exorcism. The men of the kingdom came with weapons and firearms and made a lot of noise. The ghosts were frightened and wondered if they had come to the wrong place. They said, "Now, what shall we do?" The rabbit said, "Nothing, the best thing would be to run away." They all ran into a house they just walked past. The rabbit said to the ghosts, "The royal priests have come to know of you. So you better leave this place and hide somewhere else for a few days." The ghosts sought the rabbit's advice and asked, "Where do we hide?" The rabbit said, "Just hide in those big barrels over there. The boy and I shall turn the big barrels upside down and tie them together with a rope." That's how they locked up the ghosts. The rabbit and the boy also sealed the barrels with many nails. Then they lit a huge fire and heated the barrels from below, the ghosts were helpless.

Then one day the rabbit opened a chest containing rolls of silk. He made shirts, trousers and shoes for the boy. The rabbit then said to the boy, "Now stay here. I'll bring the king's daughter to you for your wife." Then the rabbit went away. The rabbit arrived at the king's court and reported to the king, "Oh king, behind this mountain pass lives a rich man named Paṭapūli.[2] He is powerful and wealthy. I am his minister and today I was sent to ask for your daughter's hand." The king said, "Many powerful kings have asked for my daughter and I refused. I have a difficult task for you. If you could bring the skins of all the clawed beasts from this land by tomorrow morning, I'll give you my daughter." The rabbit said, "Skins we have, but I can't carry them. Please, send us one of your noble men. All the clawed beasts are like pet dogs to King Paṭapūli. If need be, I can even bring them alive to you." Then the rabbit returned to his place and addressed all the beasts, including the tigers and leopards, "Tomorrow morning,

all beasts should come to the red rocks. As I have conquered many ghosts, you will get their bodies to eat."

The next day, as morning dawned, all the beasts had assembled inside the circle of rocks. The rabbit then opened the barrels and scattered the ghost corpses all over. Some beasts enjoyed the flesh while others gnawed on the bones and then they all slept peacefully. At that time, the most trustful minister of the king arrived. He closely observed the boy and saw him attired in silk clothes and silk shoes lounging on a silk seat. Then the minister asked the rabbit, "Where are the skins of the beasts?" The rabbit replied, "They were by a tiger, all the beasts are over here, inside this area. You should catch the tiger, I'll show you where." The rabbit guided the minister to the rocks and he opened a door and said, "These are the beasts and you can catch them." The minister saw many tigers and leopards. Terrified, he could not look into their eyes and hurriedly closed the door to return to his kingdom.

The minister reported back to the king, "Everything the rabbit told you was true. The king of that kingdom is a powerful and wealthy boy with clothes, shoes and cushions made of five kinds of silk. All the beasts live in his courtyard." The king thought that other kings have silk and wealth, but no one has silk shoes and beasts in his courtyard. Therefore, I should definitely give my daughter to this king. Thus, the king gave his daughter to Paṭapūli and at a grand wedding they were happily married.

Later in time, King Paṭapūli had a son. The rabbit thought, "These three are humans, while I am a rabbit. Eventually, this son will grow up. Can I be sure that the king will still be kind to me?" The rabbit planned to test the king's reaction. So, he pretended to be sick and almost dead. He slept all day and refused to eat and sometimes did not even talk. King Paṭapūli said, "Dear rabbit, it is too bad that you've fallen ill. I am truly worried. What can I do for you? Should I go and find a physician?" The rabbit said, "No human physician can cure my sickness. If you go to the upper valley, on the shady side of the high pass you will come to a small cave. There lives a rabbit physician, whose appearance resembles mine. Show him my urine sample, he might help. I will tell you how to climb uphill through the rocks and descend into the meadows." After King Paṭapūli had left, the rabbit sprang up and dashed through the soft meadows. He reached the cave and got there before the king. Later the king arrived and reported the rabbit's condition. The doctor said, "There is one remedy to cure the rabbit. If you could kill your son and give his warm heart, only then the rabbit would recover."

King Paṭapūli returned through the soft meadows. It took him a long time to get back, as his shoes slipped off his feet in the grass. The rabbit sped down through the rocks and went back into his bed. As soon as King Paṭapūli arrived, he saw his queen carry his son on her back. He took a knife to take out his son's heart. The rabbit saw this and quickly said, "What are you doing?" The king replied, "The doctor told me that nothing can save you from death except my son's heart. You have been extremely kind to me and I cherish your life more than my own." The rabbit was fully convinced and thought that the king was indeed a nice man. The rabbit said, "Don't kill your son, now I am fine." Hence, he did not let the king kill his own son.

Thus, King Paṭapūli, the rabbit, the queen and their son became very close. They enjoyed the inexhaustible wealth of the ghosts and attained glory.

Prince Gautamiputra unmindfully remarked, "That boy and the rabbit were indeed very close and lucky too!" The Siddhivad corpse slapped the prince and escaped, saying, "The unfortunate prince uttered a word."

Here ends the fifth Siddhivad corpse story, King Paṭapūli.

1. Tib. Gtor ma (Pron. Torma, Skt. Bali) is cake prepared during ritual ceremonies.
2. Tib. Dar lham can (Skt. Paṭapūli), means one with silk shoes.

6 Śūnyatā Singha

Once again, Prince Gautamiputra carried the Siddhivad corpse from Śītavana cemetery. After they covered a long distance, the corpse said, "We are both tired and the journey is long. Either you tell me a story and I'll listen, or you raise your head and I'll tell you a story." The prince raised his head and continued listening.

The Siddhivad corpse then narrated the following story:

Once in a prosperous country lived a man named Śūnyatā Singha,[1] who lived all by himself. One day, he borrowed a donkey, loaded it with wheat and other provisions and set forth in search of a living. That evening, as he reached the border area of another kingdom he stayed as a guest at a house of an old couple. As they sat for their dinner, he said to the old couple, "My donkey and your bull are tied next to each other. The donkey may attack the bull." The old couple said, "We don't think so. We have never heard of a donkey attacking a bull." He said, "But my donkey is a special one and it might attack the bull." He pretended to go to the toilet, but instead, he disemboweled the bull with his knife and he applied blood on the donkey's ears and crept back inside and into a bed to sleep.

The next morning, Śūnyatā Singha woke up early and went downstairs. Suddenly, he cried, "Alas! This is very bad. My donkey has attacked and killed the bull last night." The old couple said, "Now, we are helpless. The old man is unable to butcher the bull, so you have to help me do it." While the old woman and the man were cutting up the bull, Śūnyatā Singha said to the old woman, "My roasted flour[2] bag is over there behind the old man. There is a possibility that the old man will eat my roasted flour. I have no objection to this, but there is the danger of the old man dying by suffocation caused by eating the dry flour." The old woman said,

"My old man will never steal flour and moreover, I have never heard of someone dying of suffocation by eating just flour." The man said to her, "Fine."

When they had finished slicing up half of the bull, Śūnyatā Singha pretended to go to the toilet. He went upstairs to the old man and killed him by suffocating him. He left an empty flour bag near the old man and sprinkled some flour on the old man's mouth, nose and hands, then he went back downstairs to continue working on the bull. After cutting up the bull, Śūnyatā Singha walked upstairs and the old woman also walked with him. She found her husband was dead with traces of white flour on his mouth. The old woman realized her mistake, but it was too late. She said, "I need help, as I can't find anyone else, you must help me carry the old man's body. I'll pay you highly for carrying the corpse." They then talked about what the payment will be for helping her.

The next day, Śūnyatā Singha went to carry the corpse, but he pretended to be unable to move it up. So he said, "Good gracious, How heavy!" He made it look like he tried to, but he could not carry the dead body. He said, "I can't carry this corpse, unless you cut off the penis." The old women said, "Please, don't say that. Just carry the body, as the weight of the penis makes no difference. Don't cut the penis, I'll pay you even more money." She also offered to give him more of the meat that she had. So, trailing a bull and a donkey behind him, Śūnyatā Singha carried the old man's corpse. When he was beyond the sight of the old woman, he placed the corpse on top of the bull. He stopped in the middle of a bridge and he made the corpse sit upright on the bill with stones from the sides. With a threaded needle placed in the corpse's left hand, it looked like an old man was stitching up the tattered rips of his Chuba.[3] Śūnyatā Singha then went away to hide and waited and watched.

After a while, a trader walked towards the bridge with many Dzo[4] loaded with tea bricks. One of the Dzo pushed the corpse and the body fell down over the side of the bridge into the river. Śūnyatā Singha quickly came back and cried, "You killed my father,

I'm reporting this matter to the king." Then he pretended to leave. The trader pleaded to the man, "Please, don't go to the king. I'll pay compensation for your loss." He demanded from the trader, "You must give me gold equal in weight to the corpse." Fearing the king's punishment, the trader paid the gold that was equal to the weight of the corpse. Śūnyatā Singha then took the gold and left that place.

Then on the outskirts of a city, Śūnyatā Singha let his donkey walk into a farmer's pea field with the corpse loaded on the donkey, then he hid himself. The donkey grazed in the field feeding on the peas. The field owner shouted many times, saying, "Don't let that donkey graze in my field! Shoo! Shoo!" However, the ignored farmer became very angry. He came and hurled a stone at the donkey. As the donkey ran away and the corpse fell to the ground, Śūnyatā Singha again came out from hiding and said, "You killed my old father. I can pay you for the handful of peas the donkey ate, but my dead father won't come back to life again." He prepared to take the case to the king for compensation. The farmer said to him, "Please, don't report this matter to the king, I will pay you." He got a hefty amount of compensation from the farmer. Then Śūnyatā Singha packed the corpse in a box and tied it with a rope. He sealed the knot with various stamps and carried it on his back. He roamed around to all parts of the city saying, "Buy sacred scriptures! Sacred scriptures!" His customers could not decide on a mutually agreeable price, so he did not sell anything from the box.

At that time, a royal attendant of the king of the land told his king that, "There are sacred scriptures for sale!" The king was curious and asked to see the man. The king asked him, "What are they for? How much is your asking price?" He replied, "The scriptures are mostly on Indian and Tibetan arts and many wealthy traders have affixed their seals. If you buy this box today and open it next year, when it is warm, you will find many artifacts. Many people wanted to buy this, but they could not afford to pay." The king asked, "How much do you want?" He said, "I want silver equal to the weight of the box." Seeing many seals affixed on the knots of the box, the king thought that they should be very sacred and priceless. Driven by sheer curiosity and greed, the king hurriedly paid silver equal to the weight of the box. Then as the warm summer was ending, the box started releasing a foul smell. The king opened and checked inside the box. There was nothing there except for a decomposed corpse. The king felt cheated, but could do nothing. The man took the silver and arrived at the place where his deceitful friends lived. He stayed there for some time. Then, as a result of his bad Karma, he caught a fatal disease and died.

Prince Gautamiputra said, "It happened because of the result of the bad Karma to Śūnyatā Singha." The corpse said, "Oh, the unfortunate prince uttered a few words, I will not stay, I will fly away." Then, the Siddhivad corpse fled the place, as before.

Here ends the sixth Siddhivad corpse story, Śūnyatā Singha.

1. Tib. Stong nyid seng ge (Skt. Śūnyatā-singha), means 'empty' lion, or foolish lion.
2. Tib. Rtsam pa (Pron. Tsampa, Skt. Sattu) is flour procured through grinding of roasted cereals such as barley, oat and maize.
3. Tib. Phyu pa (Pron. Chuba), a traditional Tibetan robe worn by both men and women.
4. Tib. Mdzo (Pron. Dzo), a hybrid of a bull and a female yak.

7 The Horse Keeper Who Never Lied

Once again, Prince Gautamiputra brought the corpse from Śītavana cemetery. The corpse said, "The journey is long and we are both tired. Either you tell me a story or raise your head so that I can tell you a story." Without uttering a word, the prince raised his head and listened.

The Siddhivad corpse then narrated the following story:

Once there was a powerful king, who ruled over his wealthy kingdom. The king had a favorite horse named Suryavadana[1] that he dearly loved. The king had many other fine horses as well that were looked after by a young horse keeper. His name was Amṛṣajña[2] and he never lied under any circumstances. There was another king in a neighboring territory who ruled on the back side of the mountain. Every year this king organized a local festival on his side to satisfy a local deity. In the spring the two kings met to watch the celebrations and to offer their prayers. They also took pride and boasted about their kingdoms.

On one day of the festival, the two kings were doing their celebration prayers for god and enjoying boasting about their kingdoms. The king who had the horse, Suryavadana, said, "We have a young man named Amṛṣajña, he is a horse keeper who never lies." The king from the back side of the mountain said, "You must be lying, as there could never be a person who never lies." The king who had Amṛṣajña working as his horse keeper said, "It is indeed true, our boy doesn't know how to lie." The other king thought of an idea and said, "If it is true, that he never lies, in seven days from now, we will meet here at the festival again. Bring your horse keeper and we can test if he can lie or not. If he can't tell a lie, I'll give my kingdom and my subjects to you. But if he tells a single lie, I'll take your kingdom and your subjects." Thus, the two kings made a bet and then they left the festival and returned to their palaces.

The next day, the king from the other side of the mountain decided to influence Amṛṣajña, the man who never lies. As Amṛṣajña left to take the king's horses to graze, the king enticed his wife to visit his kingdom on the other side of the mountain. There, the wife was lavished with splendid food and drinks. The king gave her a large basket of gold dust and told her the entire story. The king said to Amṛṣajña's wife, "Just pretend to be seriously ill. When your husband asks about the best possible remedies, tell him that only the heart of his king's favorite horse, Sūryavadana, could cure your illness. Make your husband kill that horse and ask for its heart. Tell your husband to lie and report to his king about his horse being killed by a wolf." The wife said, "No problem," then she returned to her home.

That evening, the horse keeper's wife faked an illness and lied down in her bed. Amṛṣajña asked, "How are you feeling? Is there anything that will help you?" The wife said, "Only the heart of your king's horse Sūryavadana, can help me." Amṛṣajña said, "I would give my life for you, but I can't kill my king's horse. What do I do now? We were born on the same day and we grew up together. The horse had been an immense benefit for me." The wife, in a sad tone, said, "Now, nothing can cure me and I will surely die." She pretended that she was about to die and remained motionless. After three days, Amṛṣajña went to see his king's horse Sūryavadana. The horse was in a deep sleep after having been fed with hay and water. Seeing the horse, he shed tears to express the trouble he was in. Sūryavadana woke up and asked, "My boy, why you are crying?" Amṛṣajña said, "My wife is dying and nothing can cure her. She needs your heart. You are my long time friend and I cannot kill you. Moreover, you are my king's favorite horse. I am crying because I am extremely depressed about this." The king's horse Sūryavadana said, "Don't cry, I don't have the slightest hostility for you, even if you want to kill me. To fulfill your wife's desire, just kill me, go ahead and take my heart and give it to your wife." The horse acted as if he was eager to help Amṛṣajña and part with his life. Amṛṣajña killed the horse, got the heart and gave it to his wife. The wife pretended to have an immediate recovery. Amṛṣajña thought, "Now my wife is cured but the king's horse is no more and I can't report this to

my king." He became very sad again. Because everyday, whenever Amṛṣajña went to his king, the king would always say the same thing to him, "Welcome Amṛṣajña! Are all my fine horses and my favorite horse, Sūryavadana doing well?" Amṛṣajña was worried that the king would ask this again and he feared how he should respond to his king.

Amṛṣajña had never lied before, but he thought of lying on that day, at least one time. He gathered up some stones from the meadow. He put them in a pile that stood tall like a person. He covered them with his over coat and placed his hat on top of the pile. Visualizing the pile of stones as his king, he spoke the words his king would say to him, "Welcome, young Amṛṣajña. Are all my fine horses and my favorite horse, Sūryavadana doing well?" Amṛṣajña replied to the stones, "Oh! King, not well, Sūryavadana has been killed by a wolf." The pile of stones fell down. He again piled them up to simulate the king standing there and said, "Oh! King, Sūryavadana has died." The pile of stones again fell down. He thought something must have gone wrong. Again he piled the stones up and said, "The horse Sūryavadana was lost." The stones tumbled down again. This time, he decided to speak the truth and he piled up the stones again. Visualizing them as his king and copying his king's voice, he said, "Welcome, young Amṛṣajña. Are all my fine horses and my favorite horse, Sūryavadana doing well?" He replied, "Oh! King not well. My wife fell ill and almost died. She told me that no medicine could cure her, the only cure was for her to eat the heart of Sūryavadana. I could not kill the horse, but the horse urged me to kill it and that I must not worry. Then I killed the horse and fed the heart to my wife. Now I have my wife, but not your horse anymore. May I be properly punished for my crime." As he told this story, the pile of stones remained still. Therefore, he was convinced that honesty is indeed the best way.

On the seventh day, the two kings met again at the festival and each sat on a high silver throne surrounded by their subjects and everyone enjoyed a wholesome feast. Someone informed the kings that young Amṛṣajña would be arriving there shortly. When he was before the two kings, the king from the other side of the mountain said to Amṛṣajña, "Welcome young man, are all of your king's fine horses and your king's favorite horse Sūryavadana, doing well?" The horse keeper replied, "Oh! King, not well. My wife fell ill and nothing could help her. She told me that only Sūryavadana's heart could cure her illness. I was compelled to kill the horse and feed its heart to my wife. Now, I am willing to endure any punishment my king may order." Amṛṣajña's king said, "Although, it is impossible to find another horse like my Sūryavadana on the face of this earth, it is equally rare to find a truthful young man who never lies."

Amṛṣajña's king said to the other king from the back side of the mountain, "Oh king, you have lost your bet. Now you have to give me your kingdom and all of your subjects." The king was helpless and hence gave his kingdom and his subjects away. The young horse keeper was appointed the regent of that kingdom and both the king and his ministers enjoyed happiness as infinite as the limitless of space.

Prince Gautamiputra said, "Is it true that there could be somebody who never tells a lie?" The corpse said, "The unfortunate king uttered a word, I'll not stay here anymore." Then, the Siddhivad corpse flew away.

Here ends the seventh Siddhivad corpse story, The Horse Keeper Who Never Lied.

1. Tib. Nyi ma'i gdong can (Skt. Sūryavadana), literally means one with a sun[-like] face.
2. Tib. Sdug rdzun mi shes (Skt. Amṛṣajña), means one who never spoke lies.

8 The Partridge Who Avenged Her Chicks' Death

Once again, Prince Gautamiputra returned to Śitavana cemetery and carried the Siddhivad corpse on his back. The corpse said, "Our journey is long and we are both tired. Either you tell me a story and I'll listen or raise your head and listen to me. I'll tell you a story." Not uttering a single word, the prince raised his head and listened.

The Siddhivad corpse then narrated the following story:

Long ago, in a small countryside lived a partridge that made a nest underneath a small thorny bush. A fox came and asked her, "Why are you living here?" The partridge replied, "I have made this nest of thorns for my chicks' safety." The fox said, "Then let us make a nest together and I'll help you protect your chicks from other beasts and birds of prey." The partridge believed this to be true and said, "Right, let us do that." They built a bigger nest and lived together.

One day, the partridge laid a few eggs and set them on one side of the nest. The partridge went away into the mountains in search of food. The fox ate all the eggs, except one. The partridge came to learn that the fox had eaten her eggs and was very sad. She sat there thinking about how to avenge the death of her chicks.

One day, the partridge said, "Dear friend Fox, today we must go to see a wonderful and amazing place." The fox said, "If there is such a wonderful place, we must go." They went to the lower valley and at the bottom of a hill they arrived in a field. There they saw an old man and woman tilling their land. The partridge said to the fox, "Just stay in this field, I'll make fun of the old man and woman." The partridge sat on the old woman. The old man became angry and cried, "Shoo! You ominous bird." He held a stick high to hit the partridge. The small partridge ducked and the stick missed the partridge, but it hit the old woman. She shrieked and died. Both the fox and the partridge were amused by this and laughed together.

Then the next day, the partridge said, "Today let us go to a scary place." The fox said, "Yes, let's go." They left and arrived at the house of a family. The partridge said to the fox, "Go to the courtyard and keep watching. I'll go to the roof." The partridge went to the roof and perched herself on the chimney. The members of the family walked out of the door wielding sticks and stones saying, "It is that ominous bird!" Then seeing a fox in the courtyard, they chased the fox shouting, "Hit him! Kill him!" The fox was very scared, but was able to escape. The family thought that the fox intruded into the area everyday and said, "We should lay a trap on the path." So, they laid a trap. The partridge watched the path and saw where they set the trap.

The next day, the partridge said to the fox, "Two days ago, we laughed and last night, we frightened ourselves. So today, let us go to a place where there are many types of tasty and delicious food to eat." They went to the place where the family had laid their trap. The fox hesitated and said, "I can't go there, as they've set a snare." The partridge said, "It is not meant to trap you. Don't be afraid, and there are many things to eat." The partridge walked through the trap and fed on the grains, cheese, sweetened cheese, and other food littered on the ground. She also brought back some food for the fox as well. Due to the lightness of her body, the snare did not close on the partridge, even after she walked back and forth several times. The fox thought that maybe it was not a trap. The fox wanted to eat the butter, cheese and other good things. As he sneaked up alone on the path, the trap clicked and caught a foot of the fox. The partridge watched from behind a bush and was very happy. In a terrified tone, the fox yelped, "Woah, Woah!" The old man heard the fox cry "Woah, Woah!" and he quickly came with a huge club to kill the fox.

The partridge shouted at the fox for his misdeeds and said, "Evil friend Fox, you killed my children. I have kept vengeance

in my mind and this is my revenge. Don't wag your tail, as the old man will soon be here with a club." The fox regretfully cried, "I did know that the fruit of my actions will ripen in the future, but not so soon. Woah, Woah!" The old man beat the fox to death. Despite her petite physique, the partridge was determined to avenge the death of her children.

Prince Gautamiputra remarked, "Even a partridge could take her revenge from a fox. So, one must not bully others just because they are smaller or weaker." The corpse screamed, "Oh, the unfortunate prince uttered a few words, I will not stay, I will fly away." As before, the Siddhivad corpse fled the place.

Here ends the eighth Siddhivad corpse story, The Partridge Who Avenged Her Chicks' Death.

9 The Cattle Herder Who Became a King

Once again, Prince Gautamiputra returned to Śitavana cemetery and stood at the foot of the tree, where the Siddhivad corpse was. The prince shouted, "Either you come down or I'll cut this old tree." The corpse pleaded, "Please, do not cut the old tree. I will come down." The prince put the corpse in the bag, tightened it with a rope, flung it on his back and walked for two days. The corpse said, "Our journey is long and we are both tired. Either you tell me a story and I'll listen or raise your head and listen, I'll tell you a story." Not uttering a single word, the prince raised his head and listened.

The Siddhivad corpse then narrated the following story:

Once there lived a powerful king, who ruled over a great kingdom. The king had a tall man who was his cattle herder. Everyday, the cattle herder drove the cattle to the side of a lake and then he slept on the shore of the lake. One time, he saw a hawk carrying a snake.[1] The cattle herder thought, "What a pity! I must save that snake. He threw his felt hat in the air towards the hawk and tried to do other things. Finally, the hawk dropped the snake, which fell on the shore of the lake. The cattle herder picked up and examined the snake, the snake was almost dead. He thought that if the snake died, he would roast and eat it. However, as he had saved the snake's life, he thought it was inappropriate to kill it. He wrapped the snake in his felt hat and set it aside. In the evening, when it was time to drive the cattle home, the snake said, "You are a good man. You saved my life. Please drop me into the lake and I shall repay your kindness." The cattle herder released the snake into the lake.

The cattle herder returned home that night and told everything to his neighbor, who was a wise old woman. The old woman said, "Good, you saved the snake's life. If the snake you released in the lake today is white, it must be Nāga Nṛpaśukla.[2] Tomorrow, as you go to the lake, the snake will appear and say to you, 'I owe you for your kindness.' He will bring splendid things like money and good food from the Nāgas. Do not take anything. Instead, ask for the spotted puppy that is near the door. The puppy is the Nāga's daughter and later, you shall get everything you desire." The next day, the cattle herder sat near the shore of the lake, grazing the cattle. He heard a faint call from the lake saying, "Noble one, enter the lake for a while, for I shall repay your kindness." He closed his eyes and without hesitation entered the lake and arrived at the Nāga's palace. There he saw a palace filled with treasures. There was an extremely handsome boy wearing a white silk turban who sat on a golden throne with cushions made of five different kinds of silk. He sat on a throne made of gold and white skin, like the skin of the white snake that he saw yesterday. The cattle herder sat down to the left side of the golden throne on a cushion made from exquisite silk and was offered delicious food.

The Nāga king said, "I am the Nāga king Nṛpaśukla. Yesterday, when I went to see the landscape of Tibet, I was seized by a powerful Garuḍa.[3] I could have died if you had not saved me. Please take as much wealth, food or anything you want, I shall eagerly give it to you." The cattle herder said, "I don't want anything, except for the small spotted puppy near the door." The Nāga king said, "This small spotted puppy is not meant to be given away. Oh noble one, you saved my life, so I shall give it to you." The king leashed the spotty puppy and handed it to the cattle herder. The Nāga king said, "Now close your eyes." Instantly, the cattle herder found himself out of the lake. Then the cattle herder took the puppy and drove the cattle from the shore and he returned home. He tied the puppy near the fireplace. He thought, "I arrived at the Nāga's palace and was asked to choose any wealth I wanted. However, as I was told by my old neighbor to choose the spotted puppy, I did that. Now I have nothing, but this dog. What do I do with this dog?" Suddenly, from inside the dog, a beautiful and lovely girl emerged. She was dressed in a costume studded with precious jewels and covered in ornaments of pearl, coral and white and red amber. She said, "Don't be sad. We can generate wealth and prosperity for ourselves." The cattle herder kept doing what he always did each day, he went outside with the palace cattle. The girl stayed home and she prepared all sorts of food in their house.

One day, the cattle herder thought, "In the past, when I was the king's cattle herder, all I ate was bangche,[4] I lived a hard life. Now with this Nāga girl, I have everything to eat, so I should stop working as the king's cattle herder." He told this idea to her but she had another idea. She told the cattle herder that she was the Nāga king's daughter, Avadyāna Kāntimati[5] and she had special magical powers. Then she said, "We will remain as wife and husband and we will have abundant food to eat and clothes to wear. But you should go to tend the cows and perform your duty as in the past." Like a beggar finding a precious gem, he refused to do this and he stayed home. To keep people from finding out, the Nāga girl would enter the puppy skin and become a puppy again. One day, as the girl went to fetch water, the cattle herder thought, "My wife is such a beautiful woman. Yet others see her only in a dog skin. Her beauty cannot be a match for any other human being. Therefore, he burned the dog skin. When the girl returned home, she asked, "Where is my skin?" He told how he burned it. She said, "You have not done the right thing. Now I am helpless, as I cannot perform magic anymore." They stayed as husband and wife and became richer and richer.

The king thought, "My cattle herder was a good man. However, after he got a wife, he changed and is disobedient. He has also amassed a lot of wealth and food. Now, I must ask him about his secret, about his becoming so wealthy." The next day, the king sent a messenger to summon him. Hearing what the king wanted, he said to his wife, "The king has summoned me. I must go." The girl said, "You refused to serve the king and herd his cattle. You also burned my dog skin. So there is nothing you could do. Anyway, go to the king's palace. The king may ask you to play and take a bet, but do not oblige him. Instead, listen to whatever the king orders." Then the cattle herder went to the king. The king said, "I made you my cattle herder. Now I hear that you have become very rich. So, tomorrow at sunrise, you should invite me and my ministers for breakfast." He said, "I will do the honor." Then he returned home.

The next day, the king and ministers arrived at the home of the cattle herder. The couple offered them a very grand feast, but his wife put on shabby clothes and applied soot to her face. The king stayed there for a long time and the heat from the fire warmed up the home. The wife had sweat rolling down her face and as she cleaned it with her hand, her beauty showed up from underneath the soot. The king thought of taking her for his wife. As the king knew of the laws of marriage, because he made them, he could not take the cattle herder's wife away. He wanted to take the beautiful woman away by gambling for her. The king said, "Your feast was very nice, but tomorrow morning we will come here again. At that time you should arrange for three things that I can have wherever I should point my finger." The king then left their home. The girl said, "Tomorrow you should hang up our old neighbor's shoe above the door, tie my underpants on the stairs and tie the red female dog to the stairs."

He did what his wife suggested and they stayed home waiting for the king to come back.

The next day, the king arrived at the door and shouted, "Take away that red dog from the stairs." The cattle herder pretended not to hear him and said, "What?" The king immediately pointed his finger to the dog and said, "What is this? Just take the dog away." The cattle herder took the dog away and said, "This is the first time you pointed your finger." Then the king pointed his finger towards the wife's underpants on the stairs and said, "Remove that too." He replied, "This is another finger pointing." Then, when the king climbed up the stairs and saw the shoe hanging above the door. The king said, "Take that away!" The cattle herder again pretended as if he did not hear. The king pointed towards the shoe. The cattle herder said, "This is the third time you pointed your finger at something." The king was disappointed and returned to his palace.

The king said to the cattle herder, "Now let us bet for your wife and my kingdom. You should agree to this. Tomorrow at sunrise, scatter a bag of oil-seeds in my field, we shall compete at

collecting the seeds. Either you will lose your wife or I'll lose my kingdom." The cattle herder told about this bet to his wife. She said to him, "Go to the lake and shout that the king has asked you to do gambling. Plead to the lake to lend you a box containing small birds. Once in the field, open the box and the birds will collect many seeds." He went to the lake and called out, "Please, lend me the bird box." A small box appeared on the surface. He took the box to the king's field and opened it. The box contained small birds and within a few moments, most of the seeds were collected. The king was there too and he ordered all his subjects to collect seeds, but they managed only one bagful.

Again the king said, "Next morning, at sunrise, we will have a yak[6] fighting contest. Whoever wins, will get your wife or the kingdom. The cattle herder told this to his wife that evening. She said, "The king may repeatedly tempt you. The king should also keep to his word and must ask only three times as was decided between you and him. So, tell him that you will oblige his order, but only for the last time. Tomorrow early morning, you go to the lake and say, 'Take back the bird box and please lend me the old blind yak.' " He did this and an old blind reddish brown yak appeared. He took the yak to the king. He then said, "I did everything you ordered in the past and I won. Yet you refused to give your kingdom to me. This time if I win again, you must give me your kingdom." He said what he was told to say by his wife. The king promised to do so. The king brought about 100 yaks and the cattle herder sent his old yak to challenge them. The old yak killed many of the king's yaks, many of them ran away and the others fell down, so the cattle herder won.

However, the king was reluctant to part with his kingdom and said, "Now let us bet just this one last time. This time, whoever wins will be the winner. Therefore, tomorrow at sunrise, we will meet, I with my army of one thousand armored men and whoever wins will get either the wife or the kingdom. Let us see who wins." The cattle herder thought, "Until now, I won. The king has one thousand soldiers and I have none. Now the king is using his subjects to defeat me and he will surely take away my wife." He nervously returned home and as before, he told everything to his wife. His wife said, "Don't be frightened. Return the old yak to the lake and ask for the army box. You will get a small box, but do not open it. You can then defeat the king." He did what she said and he received a small box. He took the box near the palace gate. The king had arranged for many soldiers. However, when he opened the small box, more than ten thousand soldiers came out of the box, shouting, "Where do we strike? Who do we hit?" He was frightened and said, "Hit the earth, hit the stones, hit the king, hit the palace, and hit the soldiers!" The soldiers did what was requested and soil and stones turned upside down, destroying the palace and destroying both the king and all of his soldiers. His wishes fulfilled, the cattle herder returned the box to the lake.

The couple ruled the kingdom, constructed a nine-storey palace with a gilded roof decorated with big and small musical bells. The kingdom became more prosperous than before. Through the kindness of the Nāga's daughter, people experienced happiness beyond description.

Prince Gautamiputra said, "Oh! Indeed, how fortunate was that man!" The corpse said, "The unfortunate prince spoke a word. Now I will not to stay." The Siddhivad corpse flew away.

Here ends the ninth Siddhivad corpse story, The Cattle Herder Who Became a King.

---

1. Tib. Sbrul (Pron. Drul), translated as snake, as this is considered to be one of the few forms assumed by the Nāgas according to Indic mythology.
2. Tib. Mi mgon dkar po (Skt. Nṛpaśukla), literally meaning the white lord of man.
3. Tib. Khyung chen (Skt. Garuḍa), a giant bird found in Hindu mythology and used as mount by a principal Hindu god Viṣṇu.
4. Tib. Sbang phye, flour made from residue of fermented barley used to make wine or beer. The flour from the fermented residues were mostly used as fodder.
5. Tib. Ya gar mdzes ldan (Skt. Avadyāna Kāntimati), meaning the beautiful one.
6. Tib. gyag, pronounced Yak, is a high altitude domestic cattle found in Tibet. The male species are called Yak, and the female as Dri (Tib. 'Bri; Pron. Dri).

10 Lakṣasūrya and Her Previous Lives

Prince Gautamiputra climbed to the top of a huge tree to find what tree the Siddhivad corpse was in. When he saw the corpse, the corpse cried out, "Please, don't take me." The prince climbed down from the tree and was with many smaller corpses standing around him. They each pleaded, "Please, take me." The prince drew out his sword and said, "I am Prince Gautamiputra and Nāgārjuna is my master. Come down or do you want me to cut down this tree?" As the Siddhivad corpse climbed down, Prince Gautamiputra struck the corpse with his hammer, put the corpse in the bag, tied it with a rope and carried the bag on his back. Having barely taken seven steps, the corpse called out, "Prince, Prince! Either you tell me a story or I'll tell you one." The prince recalled his teacher's advice, that he should not speak to the corpse, so he kept quite. The Siddhivad corpse said, "The unfortunate prince will not talk. Now, listen to me and I'll tell you a story."

The Siddhivad corpse then narrated the following story:

In the upper part of a kingdom, there was a king. Among his subjects, there was a rich man's son and a beggar's son. Above the valley in that kingdom, there lived a girl named Lakṣasūrya.[1] She was born very wise because she had remembered many of her previous births.[2] However, she had never spoken to a man.

One day, the rich man's son and the beggar's son met with the prince to make a bet about this girl. These three sons bet that if the prince could make her talk, he will get half of the wealth from the rich man's son. If the rich man's son could make her talk, he will get half of the kingdom from the prince. On the other hand, if the humble beggar's son could make her talk, he will get half of the kingdom from the prince and all of wealth from the rich man's son.

One day, the prince was all dressed up in his royal clothes with his ornaments. He was accompanied by his ministers and they rode elephants decorated with jewels to where Lakṣasūrya lived. The prince sang, danced and did other amusing things to impress the girl. However, she refused to say a word and the prince left. The next day, the rich man's son came, he too was wearing exquisite clothes with many ornaments that showed off his wealth. He tried to impress the girl and make her talk, but she refused. So, he returned home.

The day after that, the beggar's son left to walk up to the upper valley. He was dressed in his tattered clothes and with only half a hat hanging on his head. On the way, he met an old woman, who asked him, "Where are you going?" He replied, "Madame, I am going to talk to that girl in the upper valley who has never spoken to any man." The old woman with a condescending laugh told him to go back. She said, "Two days earlier, a prince came with many ministers on decorated elephants loaded with various things. They performed songs and danced to entertain her, but he could not make the girl speak to him. Yesterday, a rich man's son who has an enormous amount of wealth came on his best horse. He too returned without any positive reply from that girl. How can a beggar's son like you, make her talk?"

The beggar's son said, "Madam, if the girl did not talk to a prince, his ministers or to a rich man's son, does that mean the girl is dumb?" The old woman said, "How can the girl be dumb? In all of her previous births, she had created beautiful objects representing the body, speech and mind of Buddha Amitāyus.[3] Hence, she has become beautiful and she can talk very elegantly. She can remember many past lives and possesses a gentle character." The beggar's son said, "No one is greater than the king of this kingdom. Not to talk to a prince means she is even worse than being dumb." The old woman became furious and said, "Listen, the girl remembers her previous births and that is why she did not talk to them. In the past, she was once born as a tiger and hunters trapped and killed her mate with arrows. She was alone with five cubs and when she went in search of food for her orphaned cubs, hunters came and killed her cubs. When she

came back, she still stood there guarding her cubs instead of running away. The hunters killed her as well. She knew it was natural for one to suffer in this Saṃsāra. Then in her next birth, she was born as a partridge and laid her nest among the bushes. When her chicks were just about to fly, cow herders and shepherds set the bushes on fire. As she could not leave her chicks, she burned too. The male partridge tried to help her by dipping his feathers in water and flapping them to keep the fire away, but in vain. She was helpless and the entire family died in the fire. The consequence of having a family could lead to a very painful outcome. Then in her next life, she was born as a skylark. She made a comfortable nest in a rich farmer's field and laid eggs there. When the farmer plowed the land, the skylark tried to save the eggs, but again it was in vain. The farmer buried the eggs and she died also. The male skylark was hit and killed with a broom stick by the farmer when trying to rescue her. She remembers her former births very vividly and therefore does not speak to any man."

Then the beggar's son left to go to the upper valley. When he saw the girl weaving, he shouted, "Hey, you look like her!" The girl did not even care to check who was there. She just moved further away to avoid him and continued weaving. He followed her and cried, "Hey, you look like her!" The girl did not say anything, she went inside her house and securely closed the door. Again, he followed her and slept on her doorstep. He continued shouting, "Listen, you look like her. When you were born as a tiger, I went in search of food for you and was killed by hunters. You had nothing to feed the cubs. Furthermore, when you went to search for food, the hunters killed our cubs. Through your love for the cubs, you got yourself killed as well. You seem to have been that tiger. Were you not that tiger? Then, later we were born as partridges. We made a nest among bushes, which cow herders and shepherds set on fire. You were burned and I tried to put out the fire by sprinkling water with my feathers. Then, we were born as skylarks and nested in a field. When the farmer plowed the field, you and our children were all buried under the ground. When I tried to save you, the farmer killed me too. Oh,

I've been with you all through my former lives." The beggar's son was crying when he said those words.

The girl remembered her previous lives and she could not disprove what he said. She was in tears too. She opened the door and went close to him. As he repeated the stories, she said, "I remembered all my previous lives and you have been my husband in my previous lives. Why do you not come inside? Our Karmic bond has not yet ended." She invited him in and she removed his tattered rags and dressed him in nice clothes and shoes. She washed him and burned fragrant incense to make his body smell nice. From that night on, they became husband and wife.

The next day, they went to the palace. There, the king gave half of his kingdom to the beggar's son and the rich man's son parted with all of his wealth. After a few years, due to the merits they accumulated through making representations of body, speech and mind of Buddha Amitāyus, the beggar's son became the king of the kingdom. He ruled according to the Dharma and happiness and prosperity thrived in his kingdom.

Prince Gautamiputra said, "He has been very fortunate indeed!" The Siddhivad corpse said, "I finally got a reply." The Siddhivad corpse slapped the prince three times and escaped.

Here ends the tenth Siddhivad corpse story, Lakṣasūrya and Her Previous Lives.

---

1. Tib. Nyi 'bum (Skt. Lakṣasūrya), literally means as resplendent as 100,000 suns.

2. Buddhism, like many other Indian schools of philosophy, accepts the theory of rebirth or reincarnation and that your actions from your past life can determine the condition of this present life, or even the subsequent lives.

3. Tib. Tshe dpag med (Skt. Amitāyus), one of the principal Buddhas of longevity. Representation of body, speech and mind of Amitāyus include statues, Mantras and Stūpas dedicated to this Buddha.

11 The Girl Who Retrieved the King's Spirit from Death

Prince Gautamiputra seized the Siddhivad corpse as before and set forth on his journey carrying the corpse on his back. The prince said, "I am Prince Gautamiputra and Nāgārjuna is my master. The sword is Śuklacandra." The corpse said, "Oh prince! Oh prince! Our path is long. Either you tell me a story and I will listen or I'll tell you a story and you will listen." The prince did not say a word. The corpse insulted the prince by saying, "The mouth of this unfortunate prince speaks no words."

The Siddhivad corpse then narrated the following story:

Once upon a time, there lived a prince in a kingdom. Among his subjects was a young and beautiful girl whose parents had died long ago. The prince and the girl fell in love. The queen mother and her ministers discussed what to do about her son and his girlfriend. They said, "The prince should rule the kingdom and he must have a girl of noble birth and status for a queen. So we must separate the prince from his poor orphan lover." The young prince knew about how they felt about his girlfriend.

One day, the prince went to his girlfriend's house and told her, "They want me to rule over this kingdom and they have chosen a queen for me. I would rather die than marry her." The girl said, "Prince, do as your mother has advised, you must marry her, the earlier you marry the better. Before you grow too old, your son should grow up. So you must marry her now." The prince said, "If they bring me a wife, I will surely die." The girl advised, "Since your father, the king, passed away long ago, you should listen to your mother." As was planned, the prince was enthroned as the king and he then took a distant princess for his queen. A month after their wedding, the king fell ill and died.

The spirit of the deceased king traveled to the house of his former girlfriend.

One day, the king arrived at the door of his girlfriend's house, she did not know about the king's death and the king entered the house. The girl saw that his hair was unkempt and he had a withered face. She thought the king might have caught a serious illness after his marriage to his queen. She said, "Last time, you told me that you will die after your marriage and now I see a sudden loss of glow and freshness in your complexion." The king replied, "Yes, I told you that I might die, if I married another woman, but I only fell ill." She urged, "Oh king, you are ill, you must eat well and take medication. I am sure you can go back and live with the queen." The king said, "I am seriously ill. Therefore, this evening the monks are conducting a ritual for a long life. As I can see, you are bearing my child, you should come too." The girl recollected her days with the king in the past and how majestic he looked in his royal clothes and ornaments. She wondered why the king was now wearing only shabby clothes.

The girl quietly followed the king to the palace. At dusk, as they arrived at the gate, they heard the sounds of the drums and the bells coming from the palace. She said, "The drum beats are so loud that it doesn't resemble the sound made for long life rituals." The king then revealed to her, "Since you are bearing my child, my spirit is strongly attached to you. I actually died seven days ago, today they are observing the seventh day ritual." Not willing to believe that he was dead, she said, "Both your aging mother and I still love you very much, even if you have passed away." Deeply saddened, she held the king's hand and cried. The king said to her, "Don't cry, as it won't help things, let's stay together tonight." They went into a cowshed and slept there together. In the middle of the night, there was a loud commotion nearby that woke them up. They heard the king's mother and the queen quarreling. The king's mother shouted, "As soon as my son died, you hid his life bearing turquoise[1] gem and a huge amount of gold and turquoise gems. You can keep the other turquoise gems, but give me my son's life bearing turquoise gem back. It can revive him from death." The queen loudly replied, "I didn't know that his life bearing turquoise gem could cure him. It was the king who took about ten turquoise gems and the gold away, I don't understand what you are saying." They kept quarreling about this. After hearing this, the king said to the girl, "I knew that I would die. Since you have my child in your womb, I took the gold and turquoise gems from my queen to give them to you. I buried them in the middle of a drainage ditch at the corner of our field down there. I have marked the place with a pile of white stones and pebbles. Tomorrow, as the ritual concludes, you must go to my mother and tell her everything. Don't let them fight with each other. If you are brave, I will return to life." As the king heard the chanting for food offerings, he said to her, "It's time for food, now I have to go."

The king ate the food dedicated for him and came back to the cowshed with some food for the girl. She ate some of the food he brought to her. As the beats of the drums and the cymbals sounded again, the king said, "This is the prayer call for me." As he stood up to leave, the girl caught him by the bottom of his jacket and did not let him go. The king said, "It is no use holding on to me. It only makes me sadder. Convey everything that happened to my mother and you shall all live together." The girl urged him, "Just come back to see your mother, for one last time." The king replied, "I cannot see my mother, but I'll visit you on auspicious days. It will not be difficult if you remain strong and have courage." The king then disappeared into thin air.

The girl gave birth to a son in the cowshed. Overcome by her grief over the king's death and her exhaustion due to her childbirth, the girl fainted in the cowshed and remained unconscious until the next morning. At sunrise, when the cow herders came to collect the cattle, they saw the girl lying unconscious. The cow herders were frightened and reported the matter to the queen who was in the upper storey of the palace. The cow herders said, "In our cowshed is a young girl, who looked like our late king's lover. She had given birth to a child and she died with her teeth tightly closed." The queen mother dashed to the shed, lifted the girl and checked if the child was a boy or girl.

She discovered that it was a boy and she ordered the ministers, "Arrange for rice wine with molasses, sandalwood incense and flour smoke. Quickly bring them here." The ministers refused to bring the things, but she repeatedly insisted. The ministers replied to her, "We suspected such a disgraceful thing will happen one day. Moreover, this has been the reason for our king's death." The queen mother said, "This child shall take my son's place. Bring flour incense immediately." The ministers could not defy the queen mother's order. So they returned with ember, flour and juniper leaves. The queen mother made the girl and the child inhale smoke from the burned flour, massaged them with oil and gave the girl rice wine with molasses. The girl opened her eyes wide, as if rising from a deep sleep. She saw the queen mother holding her hand and she cried and fainted.

When the girl woke up, the queen mother said, "Don't cry. If there is anything I must know, just tell me." The girl said, "Please listen, Oh great queen mother! The great Dharma king told me that he would die unexpectedly if he married the queen they have arranged for him to marry. Unfortunately, I could not understand and I persuaded him to marry the queen. I did not believe that he would die if he married someone else. He asked me to get rid of this queen. Last night, the king came to my house and told me that his spirit is attached to the child. He also spent the night with me in the cowshed and sent this message for you. He revealed that he had set a pile of white pebbles on a drainage in the field. This is where he had hidden his life bearing turquoise gem and the gold. If his words are true, he said he would come to see me on auspicious days. I held on to his clothes and pleaded for him not to leave, but he would not listen. As he disappeared, I fainted." The queen mother said, "Follow me to the palace" and they escorted her there. The queen mother placed her on the king's cushion made of white felt and silk fillings. The queen mother and the ministers all concurred that they now have a prince to continue the royal lineage.

Then one full moon night, the girl heard a strange sound outside the palace. She wondered if it came from the deceased king or a devil that has come to snatch her son away. She looked out and saw the king coming. The king said, "Please, sit down." He was adorned with ivory and bone ornaments. He sat near her for a short while and he fell asleep. The girl thought, "I have told the queen mother that the king will come on auspicious days. However, she refused to believe me. This time I must take a keepsake from him. She slowly unfastened his belt and hid it under the baby's pillow. As morning dawned, the king woke up and said, "I must go, I was cautioned not to stay here." The girl told her that his belt was under the baby. "The baby might cry, I will leave it behind," said the king and left. As the sun rose, the girl went to the queen mother with the belt. She said, "The king paid a visit last night." The queen mother said, "You didn't inform me, so you must be lying. No one has ever met a dead person." The girl said, "He really had come. The belt is proof." The queen mother fainted as soon as she saw the belt. Since then, the queen mother loved the girl more than before and asked for a chance to see the king.

Again, the next full moon night, the girl heard a loud metallic sound, she knew that was when the king was arriving. She thought of informing the queen mother and sprang to her feet. The king held her and said, "Don't go. Please, sit down." She replied, "I want to bring the queen mother here." The king then said, "We manage to meet only sometimes and if you call my mother you will lose the opportunity to see me again. If you stay with my mother, there will be a chance for me to see my mother with your help, but I don't know if you will be able to help." The girl said, "If there is a way for your mother to be able to see you, I will do that even at the cost of my life." The king yelled, "Shut up!" She pleaded with him, "Oh king, for a mother, her son is as precious as her eyes. If I could make a mother meet her son and to ensure the continuation of the royal lineage, I'll do anything to accomplish it." The king told her, "If you want to accomplish this, even if it means giving up your life? Then there certainly is a way." She replied, "I'm ready to do whatever needs to be done." The king said, "Being a woman, you are not very brave and you also can't leave a baby behind. So why do this? If you think you can still sacrifice your life, then I'll tell you the way."

This is what the king instructed her to do, he said, "From here, you have to journey to the dark dungeon of devils. There is a fresh water spring. Looking at the spring, you must say that you have never seen such a dirty spring before. Drink a mouthful, then go. Walking further, you will come across a spring of puss and blood. Exclaiming that you had never seen a spring as clean as this before, take a sip and sprinkle some on your head. Keep walking and you will find yourself in front of a magnificent Stūpa. Say how ugly the Stūpa looks when walking around in an anti-clockwise direction. As you walk up to the Stūpa, you will see a mound of dog waste. Praise how holy it looks as you continue to walk. You will see an old woman roasting grains, you should give her a pair of tongs. As you walk further, you will see two naked boys. Give them clothes to wear. Then you will see two goats fighting for a bunch of grass. Give each goat a bunch of grass. Then you will see two old dogs fighting over a piece of bone. Give them each a bone. Then walk further and you will reach an iron house with four gates. You will see a devil couple wearing Tantric outfits in front of a Maṇḍala[2] that has many hearts around a circle on the Maṇḍala. All the hearts will cry out, 'Please take me,' but the smallest heart in the center will plead, 'Please don't take me.' That heart will be redder and greasier than the rest. Just bring that heart here, back to me. That devil couple in Tantric outfits are powerful and terrifying, so it will be extremely challenging for you." The girl said, "If the king could live again, I would be willing to sacrifice my life." The king said, "Have no fear. Just grab hold of that heart without turning it and put it in your pocket. Walk straight back to the palace and never look back, but I doubt if you can do that." The girl said, "These tasks may be challenging, but I'll accomplish them. I pray that the mother and son will meet again." The king again cautioned her, "Do not turn or look behind you until you reach back to the palace." The girl went to the queen mother and told what the king had instructed. The queen mother was ecstatic and asked, "When will you leave?" The girl replied, "On the 29th day of this lunar month."

On the evening of that day, the girl carried her provisions and set forth on her mission. As she reached the place where the fresh spring was, she exclaimed, "I have never seen such a dirty spring before." She went further and saw a spring with puss and blood oozing from it. She said, "I have never seen such a pure and clean water spring before." She took a sip and splashed her face. Then as she came across a magnificent Stūpa, she said, "I have never before seen such an ugly Stūpa." She then walked anti-clockwise around the Stūpa. Then she saw an ugly Stūpa, whereby she exclaimed, "I have never seen such a holy and magnificent Stūpa before" and she walked around the Stūpa. She walked further and saw an old woman roasting grains and she gave her a pair of tongs. Later she met two naked boys, whom she gave clothes to wear. Then she saw two goats and gave each a bunch of grass to eat. Walking a little further, she saw two dogs fighting and threw to them each a bone.

Finally, she reached a huge iron castle with four huge gates. She entered the castle from the eastern gate and saw someone wearing Tantric clothes and beating a drum, while others were lying nearby and chanting, "Hum Hum Phat Phat..." She felt shivers in her calves, yet moved stealthily. Without any hesitation, she grabbed hold of the heart that cried, "Please, do not take me." She tucked it securely in her pocket and ran. She reached the place where the two dogs stood. The Tantric priest seeing her flee, shook their heads in dismay and bared their fangs with fury. With seven male demons to his right and seven female demons to his left, the Tantric demon chased the girl. He shouted at the two dogs, "Catch the girl!" Those dogs were grateful for the bones she threw to them and thus cried, "Run, Run." She fled further and saw the two goats. The demons shouted, "Catch her." Those two goats, feeling grateful for the grass she gave, shouted, "Run, Run." And she escaped. Then as she reached the place where the two boys stood, the demons shouted, "Catch her." Those two boys, remembering her kind act of giving them clothes, said, "Run, Run." As she reached the old woman, the devils screamed, "Catch her." The old woman, grateful for the pair of tongs that she received cried, "Run, Run." The girl fled and then as she reached the ugly Stūpa, the demons again shouted, "Catch her." The ugly Stūpa thought, "She is the only person who sought my blessing and bowed to me," it too said, "Run, Run." Next, she arrived at the place where stood the magnificent Stūpa. The demons shouted, "Catch her," but the Stūpa let her go by without saying anything. As she ran further, she reached the spring of puss and blood. The devils shouted, "Catch her," but the spring recollected the girl's praises and said, "Run, Run." She ran and reached the place where flowed the fresh spring. The demons shouted, "Catch her." The spring said, "I don't care." Thus, she escaped.

When the girl got back and entered the palace, she came up to the king, who again said to her, "Do not look back." The king's cautioning her to never look back rekindled her curiosity and she looked back. As a result, the king suffered a minor wound in his left eye. In this way, she retrieved the heart and brought the king back to life. The king was happy to see his mother again. The queen mother and all the king's ministers were happy as well. It marked a rare meeting of the dead with those of the living. The king took the girl as his queen and later they had five children. He sent his former queen back to her father's kingdom.

Prince Gautamiputra remarked, "The girl has been truly faithful and brave as well." The Siddhivad corpse said, "The unfortunate prince spoke a word." Saying this, the Siddhivad corpse flew away.

Here ends the eleventh Siddhivad corpse story, The Girl Who Retrieved the King's Spirit from Death.[3]

---

1. Tib. Bla g-yu, literally meaning life-bearing turquoise is a turquoise, where dwells the soul of a person. Such turquoises are believed to change the power to determine the condition of life of the owner.
2. Tib. Dkyil 'khor (Skt. Maṇḍala), a traditional design of symmetrical nature, mostly resembling celestial mansion of gods and deities.
3. This story has a similar plot as the 20th story in this book.

12 The Wise King and the Three Sisters

Once again, Prince Gautamiputra walked to Śītavana cemetery and ordered the Siddhivad corpse, "Will you come down from the tree or shall I cut the tree down." The prince brandished his sword, wielded his hammer and raised his rope. The corpse descended from the tree. The prince caught the corpse, bound the corpse in the rope and put the corpse in the bag. He flung the bag on his back and then started walking. The Siddhivad corpse said, "Oh prince, as the day is long, listen to me and I will tell you a story."

The Siddhivad corpse then narrated the following story:

Once upon a time, there was a wealthy king who was of the magnificent Kṣatriya caste[1] and he ruled over a kingdom with a huge population and a vast territory. The rulers of the neighboring kingdoms were eager to offer their daughters for marriage to him. The king, however, felt it important to examine them before taking one as his queen. The king was knowledgeable and an expert in examining women.

The king came to learn that an old couple living in a neighboring kingdom had three fortunate daughters. The king thought, "If I asked for the hands of their daughters for marriage, they would willingly give them to me. However, I must check how wise and noble the three daughters are." The king changed himself into an old dog. Then carrying a sack of barley, he appeared at the door of the old couple. When the dog saw the old mother carrying a pail of water, he said, "Woof, woof. Can you keep this sack of barley for me, please?" "No problem," said the old mother. The old dog said, "When should I come back to collect this same sack of barley?" The old mother asked, "When would you like to come?" The old dog replied, "I can't say. I am not sure when I'll be able to come back" and then he went away.

For several years, the old dog did not return to collect the sack of barley. The old father said, "That was an old shaggy dog with long matted hair. Dogs live only about nine years. He could have died by now, as he did not come back to collect the sack of barley. Although he had earlier demanded that we return the same barley, we need not be that strict. So, why don't we brew wine from that barley?" The old mother said, "Yes, he told me that he prefers to have the same barley, because his is a good barley, but we can replace it with ours." Therefore, the old mother brewed wine from the old dog's barley.

Then the next day, the old dog arrived at the nearby river and met the eldest daughter, who had come to fetch water. The old dog said to her, "Woof, woof. Girl, I have come to collect the barley I left with your mother." The eldest daughter returned home and said, "Mother, the old dog has come to collect the barley." The old mother said, "Then ask him to come in." The old dog came to the house. The old mother said, "Sir, we waited until yesterday, but you didn't come. As we wanted to use the barley, we mixed your barley with ours." The old dog said, "Even if you have mixed them up, you must separate them. I want my own barley, or I won't go." "If you want it that way, why did you not come back sooner?" asked the old mother. The old dog snapped back, "Did I not tell you that I can't tell you when I'll come back? If you can't give me the same barley, you must part with your daughter." The old couple was helpless and gave him their eldest daughter.

The old dog took the eldest daughter with him. On their way, they came across a big river. The old dog said, "Woof, woof. I'll carry you on my back." As he carried the girl on his back, he knew that the girl was not very wise. The dog then took her inside a cave, where he had hidden a bed, food and drinks. The old dog said, "Eat some butter and sweetened cheese and give me some to eat. And just relax on the mattress." The eldest daughter thought that old dog liked to eat leftover food and hence put

some in the bowl while she enjoyed the meat. She then stacked up three mattresses for herself and left one for the dog. The old dog knew that the girl was not only cruel, but stupid as well. Knowing that she was one of the unlucky daughters, he decided to search for a wiser one. The old dog said to her, "Let us go back and see your mother."

The old dog and the eldest daughter returned to her mother. The old dog stayed outside the door and only the eldest daughter went into the house. The old mother asked, "Welcome daughter, were you happy?" The eldest daughter replied, "Yes, I enjoyed a lot of things, as there was enough to wear and eat." The mother then asked, "Where is the old dog?" "He's outside, mother," replied the eldest daughter. The old mother said, "Foolish girl, bring the dog in." The old dog entered the house. The old mother greeted the dog. The dog said, "Woof, woof. How do you do, old mother" The old couple served him food and drinks. The old dog said, "Can I take your second daughter?" The old mother agreed and said, "As you were nice to our eldest daughter, we will give the middle one this time."

Then the old dog left the place with the middle daughter and arrived at the river. The old dog said, "Woof, woof. Oh lady, I'll carry you on my back." The middle daughter said, "Sir, you don't need to carry me. I'd be happy if you could help me carry my clothes and shoes instead." She bundled her clothing together and loaded them on the old dog. The old dog led her to the cave as before, thinking that she is better than her elder sister. The old dog said, "Relax on the mattress, eat meat, butter and the other food. Give me some to eat too." The middle daughter gave half of the meat and half a bone to the dog and then ate until she was full. The old dog thought, "Though she is wiser than the previous one, but I must test the youngest girl." The old dog said to the middle daughter, "Let us go back to see your old parents."

The old dog carried a large piece of meat and arrived at door of the old couple. As the middle daughter went inside, the old mother said, "Welcome daughter, were you happy?" And she replied, "Yes mother, I have been happy." The old mother asked,

"Where is the old dog?" The middle daughter said, "The old dog is waiting outside our door." The old mother scolded her, "You foolish girl, bring the dog inside." The old mother invited the dog in the house and asked, "Oh my friend, so you have come back." The old dog said, "Woof, woof. How are you doing?" Then the old dog was served delicious food and drinks. The old dog said to the old mother, "Can I have your youngest daughter?" The old couple said, "No problem. We will give her to you. Our daughters have been happy to be with you."

The old dog took the youngest daughter. When they reached the riverbed, the old dog said to the youngest daughter, "I'll carry you on my back." The youngest daughter said, "You can't carry me. Even if you are a dog, my parents have given my hand to you for marriage. Now that you are my husband, you must not carry me." The old dog was pleased and said, "Then let me carry your shoes." The youngest daughter said, "It is not good to make you carry my shoes." She tied them to her waist and crossed the river. They arrived at the cave. The old dog said, "Girl, be comfortable, eat meat and butter and give me the leftovers to eat." The youngest daughter melted the butter and fried the meat. She served them to the old dog. Then she ate the leftovers. She gave a thick mattress to the old dog and used a thin one for herself. The old dog mumbled to himself, "I think this one is better than the two other girls." The youngest daughter said, "Since my mother has given me to you, I have no regrets, even if you are a dog." She cleaned up his dog waste and behaved like an obedient wife.

The old dog prayed that this intelligent girl become his spouse for life. The old dog and the youngest daughter lived in the cave for many years. In the meantime, she gave birth to several puppies. The old dog said to the youngest daughter, "This is not our real home." The youngest daughter said, "Since the puppies are too young to run, or even walk and we have many things to carry, like utensils and beds, stray dogs will surely attack us on our way home. I feel ashamed to sneak my puppies out of my home. So, we must not go at this time." The old dog said, "My friend will look after the stuff in the cave. It is possible that the village dogs can not see us and will not attack us. Let us take the chance. Put the puppies securely in your pocket and let us leave now." The old dog walked ahead, while the youngest daughter followed him. After a while, the old dog changed his disguise and began to leave human footprints on the road. When she reached the valley, she saw a dog skin, flesh and blood spread on the rocks. The youngest daughter saw it and cried, "Alas, my old dog. How unfortunate! Abandoned by my parents, I lived with this old dog. I wish we had stayed in the cave. I am now like a person possessed by a ghost. My home is far away and it is shameful to go on with fatherless puppies. I can't beg for food either." Placing her head on the dog skin, she cried and cried.

After some time, a man riding a fine horse arrived and said, "Madam?" The youngest daughter wondered who this man could be. She remained in the same position and did not rise. The horseman gripped her by her arm and said, "Please, get up." The youngest daughter said, "Gentleman, I have lost my way. My husband was an old dog. The village dogs have killed him and left his skin here." He said, "You are wrong. You don't know anything" and he took her hand. She thought, "This skin belonged to my husband, so how can I be wrong?" She stood up and looked at the man. He gave her silk clothes and ornaments to wear. He then asked, "Where are your children?" She replied, "I have no human babies, only puppies." He placed her on a golden saddled horse and many horsemen escorted her to the great palace.

There, she saw a king, wearing precious ornaments and silk clothes, seated on a golden throne. The king was surrounded by many ministers. The king asked her to sit on a throne made of turquoise gems. She thought, "I am the wife of an old dog, I can not sit on this throne." Then the king asked, "Where are your children?" The minister brought in three puppies and handed them to the king. As the king removed their skin, they changed into three handsome princes. The king said, "I changed myself into a dog only to test you." This made the girl happy. The girl paid her respects and sat on the turquoise throne. This was the way, the king examined the three daughters of the old couple and made the most intelligent one his queen.

Prince Gautamiputra exclaimed, "Oh, what a kind and intelligent girl!" The corpse shouted, "The unfortunate prince uttered a word!" Once again the Siddhivad corpse flew away.

Here ends the twelfth Siddhivad corpse story, The Wise King and the Three Sisters.

1. Kṣatriya is the second, in hierarchy, of the four conventional castes in Indian social system and includes the class of kings and warriors. The other three, in order of superiority, being Brahmaṇa priests, Vaiśya traders and craftsmen, Śūdra servants and laborers.

13 The Mother and Daughter Who Tamed the Man-Eating Tiger

Once again, Prince Gautamiputra arrived at the Śītavana cemetery and caught the Siddhivad corpse. Carrying the corpse on his back, the prince set forth on his journey. The corpse said, "The journey is long and tiresome. You should tell me a story and I shall listen. If you want me to tell you a story, raise your head." Prince Gautamiputra did not say a word.

The Siddhivad corpse then narrated the following story:

Once upon a time, there lived a tiger in a forest not far from a prosperous and growing city. Due to his previous Karma,[1] the tiger became a man-eater. The city decided to send one person as food for the tiger to kill each year. In the outskirts of the city, there lived an old mother and her daughter. One year, it was their turn to go as food for the tiger.

On the last day of a lunar month, the old mother and her daughter were talking, "We are to be eaten by the tiger tonight. So before that let us eat some food ourselves." They prepared wheat porridge and poured in it hot pure butter and began to eat. The tiger stealthily came to their house and walked through the door. As the hot melted butter overflowed from the bowl and made a crackling sound, the girl cried, "Mom, the crackle[2] has come." The tiger thought, "I heard her mention about a beast called Crackle. Who is more powerful than me? It seems that another beast has come here today." The tiger was very frightened and sat trembling behind the door.

Two thieves from the city arrived and one whispered to the other, "The old woman and her daughter must have been eaten by the tiger. We can now steal her cow." The two thieves slowly entered the compound and searched for the cow. Shrouded in complete darkness, they mistook the tiger for the cow and dragged the tiger from behind the door. Having tied a rope around its neck, one of them pulled the tiger, while the other pushed him from behind. The tiger followed meekly thinking it was the terrifying beast called Crackle doing this. The next morning at dawn, the thief pushing from behind saw that it was a tiger. He turned around immediately and ran away without looking back. The thief in front continued walking. As he approached a tree, he looked back and saw the tiger. He was very frightened, he tied the rope to the trunk of the tree and climbed to the top of the tree and waited. After a while, a fox came near the tiger and asked, "What happened? What's wrong with you?" The tiger said, "Don't talk to me, you evil fox. The ferocious Crackle tied me to this tree and is now up in the tree." The fox looked up and saw the thief. The fox said, "Oh tiger, what a fool! This is not Crackle, but a Tibetan black headed earthworm. Do not be afraid. I have an idea, just stay put." The fox then went away.

The fox gathered all kinds of animals and said, "All animals will climb on top of each other and on the tiger. I'll climb to the top and I will throw down the black headed earthworm to the ground." The thief knew it was a fox and slapped him hard three times. The fox cried loudly and the cries resounded throughout the valley. All beasts including the tiger were terrified and soon all of them fainted. Immediately, the thief climbed down the tree and tied up the fox. He then killed and skinned the other beasts. The thief was cleaning the animal hides when a merchant came by driving his caravan of dzos loaded with tea bricks. The merchant was astonished to see so many dead animals scattered around and asked, "Did you kill all the animals of the hides that you are cleaning? How did you kill them all?" The thief replied, "My red dog killed them." The merchant said, "Why don't you sell me your dog?" The thief said, "My red female dog is like a fox and can kill any beast. I don't want to sell my dog. But if you are willing to give me your dzos and your tea load, I will give you the dog." The merchant gave everything to the thief and said, "Now,

tell me how I must order the dog to kill beasts." The thief said, "Early in the morning, take this dog to a high rocky pass. Call him 'Evil Fox' and hit him three times with an empty bag and then let it loose." Then the thief took the dzos, loaded them with tea and the animal hides and left the place.

The merchant did as the thief instructed, he climbed up to a high pass and then yelled, "You, Evil Fox." Then hitting her hard with an empty bag three times he released her. He waited for three days, but the dog never came back. Thus, came our historical rhetoric: "Hitting a fox with an empty bag." The merchant was helpless and returned home. Having gained the trust of the merchant, the thief got the merchant's wealth. The thief became rich; however, due to bad Karma, he suffered a fatal illness and died.

Prince Gautamiputra then remarked, "It was actually a thief that saved the old mother and her daughter." The Siddhivad corpse said, "The unfortunate prince spoke, now I will stay no more." Then, the Siddhivad corpse flew away.

Here ends the thirteenth Siddhivad corpse story, The Mother and Daughter Who Tamed the Man-Eating Tiger.

1. Theory of causalty or action expounded in Indian schools of philosophy including Buddhism which view actions of body, speech and mind as determining the entire course of our future lives and experiences within the 'cycle of existence' called Saṃsāra.
2. Tib. Sag. Onomatopoeic word used to indicate a crackling sound. Here the tiger mistakes "Crackle" or the Tibetan "Sak" for name of a non-existent ferocious beast.

14 Masang Yarukhata, the Brave Minotaur

Once again, Prince Gautamiputra walked the same route and arrived at Śītavana cemetery. He caught the Siddhivad corpse, carried the corpse on his back and began his journey back home. The corpse said, "The day is long and we are tired. Tell me an interesting story and I will listen. If you want me to tell you a story, just give a nod." The prince did not say a word.

The Siddhivad corpse then narrated the following story:

Long ago, in a narrow valley, lived a bachelor who had nothing except for a cow. There came a time when he wanted to mate his cow with a bull. He searched all around, but could not find a bull anywhere. He was very sad and thought, "If my cow does not bear a calf, I'll not have another cow and not any butter, I'll die of hunger." He tried and looked around again, but in vain. Therefore, he mated with the cow. In due course, the cow gave birth to a minotaur, a human with a long tail and a cow's head. He was not happy with the way his calf looked, so he got his bow and aimed an arrow at the child, but the child cried, "Father! Please, don't kill me. If you save me, I'll surely repay your kindness." Then the child left for the forest in the mountains.

Once in the forest, the minotaur saw a black man sitting under a tree. The minotaur introduced himself as, Masang Yarukhata.[1] Masang asked the man, "Who are you?" The man replied, "I am Nagke Darpo.[2] Where are you going? Can I come with you?" Masang agreed and they walked together. Then they met a green person on a lush green meadow. They asked him, "Who are you?" The man replied, "I am Pangke Darpo.[3] Can I come with you?" Then the three walked together. After a while, they arrived in the center of a thick mountain forest, they saw a white man. They asked, "Who are you?" He replied, "I am Shingke Darpo.[4] Can I come with you?" The four men walked together and found themselves in a vast valley. There they found a small hut on the edge of the mountain. There was food and furniture in the house and dzomo[5] in the compound. No owner or anybody was to be seen around. So they decided to stay there. Each day, three of them went hunting, while one stayed home.

One day, Nagke Darpo was at home. He churned the curd for butter and cooked meat. Then he heard the door open and someone climbing the stairs. He wondered who this aggressive person could be. There he saw a teeny tiny woman, standing only as tall as a finger. She was carrying a basket as small as a bee. She said, "Hey boy, are you cooking something? Let me taste the curd and eat some of the meat." Just as he was about to let her taste the food, thc small woman disappeared. Nagke Darpo walked downstairs and saw that everything had disappeared, there was no curd and no meat. He was ashamed and searched the cupboards, but he only found two hooves. He used them to make horse footprints all around the house and he shot many arrows on the roof. After a while, his friends, who went hunting deer, returned. They asked, "Where is the butter from the curd and where is the cooked meat?" Nagke Darpo replied, "About 100 horsemen arrived here. They took all of our food and they beat me so badly that I could hardly move. Look at the footprints outside." They went out and checked. They saw the footprints of horses and arrow marks on the roof. They said to each other that it was true.

The next day, Pangke Darpo stayed home. The same thing happened to him and he did the same as his friend, he marked the ground with many footprints using a yak hove. He told them, "I was attacked by a brown yak."

The third day Shingke Darpo stayed at home. He too did the same thing as his friends and marked the ground with footprints using a mule hove. Then he lied, "Today, about 100 men came here riding mules."

On the fourth day, Masang Yarukhata was home while his friends left to go hunting. With his sharp pointed horns and his raised tail, he was there churning the curd. The small woman came and said to him, "Oh man, let me taste some meat and curd." He wondered if this had happened before with his three friends. Not knowing what would happen if he let the woman taste his meat and curd, he said to her, "Before I let you taste the food, you should fetch me some water." He made holes in the bottom of a barrel and sent her off to the river. As he looked through the window, the little old woman, measuring only the size of a fist, changed into a tall woman that stood as high as the sky. She repeatedly filled the barrel with water, but she found it empty. In the meanwhile, he opened her backpack and found a braided rope, an iron hammer and a pair of iron tongs. He replaced them with an old woolen rope, a wooden hammer and wooden tongs. Then the teeny tiny woman came in and said, "Your barrel doesn't hold water. If you don't let me taste the meat and the curd, all of this wealth will be mine. Let us play a game." The woman tied Masang Yarukhata up with the woolen rope, but he struggled hard and he snapped the rope. Then he tied her up with the braided rope and she could not move. She said, "You won this time. Now let us pierce each other with tongs." She struck his chest with the tongs, but he was not hurt. Then he struck her with the pair of iron tongs on her chest. He pierced her flesh, twisted it hard and took out a chunk of her flesh. She cried out in pain and said, "Ah! You are a strong man. Now let us hit each other with a hammer." She hit him hard on the chest with the wooden hammer, but the handle broke and it did not hurt him that much. He struck a heated iron hammer on her chest, head and other parts of her body. Blood oozed from everywhere on her body and she fled downstairs.

When his friends returned from hunting, they said, "Hey Masang Yarukhata, you should be tired now." In reply, Masang reprimanded, "You lowly beggars. You all lied to me and acted unmanly. I have subdued the small woman. Let's go and see her dead body." They followed the blood spots. In the crevices of a deep rocky precipice about 120 feet[6] (72 m) down, they saw her body. They also saw an inconceivable amount of wealth, including a great amount of gold, turquoise gems, armor and weapons, etc. Seeing this, Masang Yarukhata said, "You three must go down and tie the wealth to a rope and I'll pull it all up. Or I will go down and tie it up while you pull it up." They said, "This lady was a ghost and we're afraid to go there. Masang Yarukhata, you must go down instead of us." Then they lowered Masang Yarukhata down the precipice with the help of a rope. He tied all the wealth to the rope and they pulled it up. When they collected it all at the top, the three men decided to trick Masang Yarukhata. They discussed, "If we pull Masang Yarukhata out, he might take away all the wealth. So why don't we only share it among ourselves?" They left Masang Yarukhata in the deep precipice.

Masang Yarukhata learned that his three friends have deceived him and thought he would die there. He searched for something to eat and found three apricot seeds. He buried them in the soil, watered them and prayed, "If I am to survive this ordeal, may three apricot trees appear as I wake up. Or else may I die right away." He placed his head on the corpse of the woman and slept. Due to the decomposing and polluted corpse, he slept for many years. When he woke up, three apricot trees had grown with branches touching up to the edge of the precipice. He was ecstatic, he climbed up the trees and got to the top again.

Masang Yarukhata went to the house, but saw no one there. He found his iron bow and arrows lying around. He took them and went to the house where the three men lived. He saw that his three friends have each taken a wife. He asked the wives, "Where have your husbands gone?" They replied, "They went to hunt deer." Armed with an iron bow and arrows, he searched the area. Then he saw them returning home with a slain deer. He shot an arrow and injured them. They said, "You are right. Please take away our house and our wives. Spare us and we will go our own way." Masang Yarukhata said, "What you did was bad. I have to go repay my father's kindness. I'll let you live here like before." Then he went away.

From there, Masang Yarukhata met Indra,[7] the king of the gods. God Indra said, "Today gods and demons will fight against each other. All the white ones are gods and the black ones are demons. This afternoon, when the black yaks chase the white yaks, you should shoot your iron arrow at the black yak with a shiny forehead." He followed her instructions and shot the iron arrow in the forehead of the black yak. All the remaining black yaks fled for their life.

Indra was very pleased and said, "You are a nice man. Stay here for one night." But, Masang Yarukhata said, "I have to repay my father's kindness. So I must go." Indra gave him a gift of many precious stones. Indra said, "Don't make mistakes by sleeping during your journey, in case you miss the right path, you will arrive at the gate of the devil. You will not be able to escape. So, knock at the door and tell them that you are a physician. The king of the devil was hit by an arrow. If they bring him to you for treatment, just pretend that you are curing him. Then throw seven grains of barley seed into the air and push the arrow deeper into his brain to kill him."

Then he left on his journey. He diverted from the path and arrived at the gate of the devils. As he knocked at the door, a devil's daughter with flames burning from her mouth came and asked, "Who are you?" He replied, "I am a physician, and I practice medicine." She asked him, "Come in." She showed him the devil king, who was hit by an arrow. He first threw seven grains of barley and pretended to remove the arrow. Instead, he pushed the arrow deeper into the brain and killed him. At that time, Indra, the king of the gods, soared through the celestial realms with a clinking sound of an iron chain. The devil's daughter threw a burning iron ball at him and cried, "Break his waist." The iron ball missed him and became a constellation, later named Saptarishi.[8]

Prince Gautamiputra asked, "Did he succeed in repaying his parent's kindness?" The Siddhivad corpse screamed, "Oh, the unfortunate prince uttered a word! I will stay no more!" Then, the Siddhivad corpse flew away.

Here ends the fourteenth Siddhivad corpse story, Masang Yarukhata, the Brave Minotaur.

---

1. Tib. Ma gsang Ya ru kha khra, this name can be loosely translated as 'single-horned, piebald-faced secretive one.'
2. Tib. Nags skyes dar po, literally means jungle boy.
3. Tib. Spang skyes dar po, literally means boy from the grassland.
4. Tib. Shing skyes dar po, literally means wood-born lad or boy from the woods.
5. Tib. Dzo mo is a female Dzo, a common name for a crossbreed between an ox and a female dri, and is a proper name for its male species.
6. Tib. 'Dom, an ancient unit of measurement, equivalent to the length between the tips of middle finger of outstretched arms.
7. Tib. Lha dbang brya byin (Skt.Devarāja Śakra), more popularly known as Indra, is the King of Gods according to ancient Hindu mythology.
8. The Big Dipper.

15 The Diviner With the Pig-Head

Once again, Prince Gautamiputra walked the same route and arrived at Śitavana cemetery. He caught the Siddhivad corpse, carried the corpse on his back and began his journey back home. The Siddhivad corpse said, "The day is long and we are tired. Tell me an interesting story and I will listen. If you want me to tell you a story, just give a nod." The prince did not say a word.

The Siddhivad corpse then narrated the following story:

Long ago, in a very beautiful upper valley, there lived a husband and his wife. The husband was a selfish and stingy man who never spent money on food or drinks. He slept all day and night.

One day, his wife said, "Don't be so lazy. We have almost used up all the wealth inherited from your father. Now, put on your clothes and watch me while I work in the field." As his wife earnestly begged him, he got out of bed and climbed to the roof of their house. He looked down at the adjacent plot of land, which used to be a nomad's camping area. There he saw a fox and a dog fighting. He went down there and when he was there, he found a big chunk of butter and the leg portion of mutton. He brought them home and stored them in the cupboard. When his wife returned, she asked, "Where did you get the butter and meat?" He replied, "As you told me, I just climbed to the roof to take a look. I saw a fox, a few dogs and many birds. I went closer and found these things." She said, "That's why I told you not to be lazy. Look, how much you have got just by climbing to the roof." Encouraged by her words, he said to his wife, "Prepare for a journey. Arrange my horse with a saddle and straps and a white hat, a black felt jacket and a dog too." She arranged them accordingly and said, "I have arranged all these things for you. You should be ready to go."

The husband put on the white hat and the black felt jacket, carried three different weapons, mounted the horse and called the dog. Then he rode away aimlessly towards unexplored routes. As he rode further, he saw a fox. He thought, "The first catch is an auspicious occasion, it leads to more favorable opportunities." He shouted, "Stay put, you fox" and he advanced closer. The fox escaped into a narrow hole. He dismounted from his horse, put down his bow and arrows and removed his clothes and left them on the saddle. He tied the dog to the saddle. He tried to enter the hole, but he could not fit into the small opening. As he blocked the hole with his white hat, he tapped the ground with a stone. The frightened fox instantly jumped out of the hole and fled with white hat balanced on his head. The dog, that was tied to the saddle, ran after the fox and pulled the horse along too. They crossed the mountain pass and in a moment they were gone.

The husband remained there naked and helpless. He walked to the lower valley and hid himself in the haystack inside the cattle shed of a powerful and wealthy king. Covered entirely by hay, nobody could see him. After a while, a beautiful princess came out for a walk and urinated near him. She dropped the king's life bearing turquoise[1] gem, which is as dear to the king as the kingdom itself. However, the princess was unaware of the loss of the turquoise gem and she returned to the palace. As he was hiding in the haystack, he was unable to pick up the life turquoise gem. As the sun began to set, a cow defecated and the dung covered the turquoise gem. After a while, a maid servant kneaded the dung with straw into cakes and stuck them on the wall.[2]

The next day, the king and his ministers ordered the sounding of the huge drum. As all his subjects gathered, an announcer cried, "The king's life bearing turquoise gem has been lost by our princess." Then they summoned diviners, oracles and soothsayers. At that time, the husband revealed half of his body from the haystack. A man saw him and asked, "Who are you?" He replied, "I am a diviner and a soothsayer." The man said, "If you know how to discover hidden knowledge, then let us go to the king. The king's life bearing turquoise gem has been lost, all diviners of the land have gathered for this purpose." He said, "I am naked." The man went to the king and reported, "Outside our palace, there is a naked diviner. If we will give him clothes, he will appear before you." The king said, "Give him some clothes to wear. Open the gates for him and bring him here." Then he was escorted inside the palace. He appeared before the king, he paid his respect by bowing deeply to the king. Then the king asked, "What things do you need for the divination." He replied, "I need a head portion of a big pig, a staff braided in five colors of silk and a big ritual cake." The king ordered to arrange all these. He put the pig's head on a stick, attached the five color banners to it and placed it on the ritual cake. Then he pretended to be in retreat for three days and closed the door.

Then after three days, all the people of the kingdom gathered. The man put on a black costume, took the pig's head in his hand and sat on the street. He let the people pass and then pointing the pig's head on each person, said, "This one doesn't have the turquoise gem and not this one and..." Everyone was happy. Then he said, "The king's life turquoise gem is not with the people. Now I must search another area." Walking around the palace, he pointed the pig's head on every stone and on all of the king's attendants and kept searching with the musicians playing and following him. Then the husband entered the barn, where he knew the turquoise gem was. Then he pointed the pig's head on the cow dung and said, "Here it must be." The king took the cow dung off the wall and found the life bearing turquoise gem. Everyone was happy and the king said, "You are indeed a great diviner. Now we want to repay your kindness. Please come to my palace." The king said, "Hey pig-head diviner! You are great." All his subjects were pleased. The king asked him, "What reward would you like to have?" The diviner was in need of his earlier possessions, so he asked for a horse with a saddle and a harness, a white hat, a black felt jacket, a dog on a leash and a fox. The king said, "He is a very simple minded man, gave him all those

things." The king also gave him three elephant loads of meat, a cheesecake and butter.

As he returned to his village, his wife came to receive him with welcoming wine and said, "You are the ideal man." Then she invited him into their house. In the evening, they talked in their bed and the wife said, "Where did you get all the meat, cheesecake, butter, etc?" He told her everything. She said, "You are such a stupid husband with no principles. I am going to report this to the king early tomorrow morning." The next morning, his wife went to the king with a letter that she wrote pretending it was from her husband. It said, "I recovered the king's life bearing turquoise gem and dispelled a bad omen. To dispel that bad omen, I asked for only a dog, a fox, etc. What reward do I truly deserve for finding the life turquoise gem is for the king to decide." As she handed the forged letter to the king, he said, "He is right," and gave her many more things. The diviner then lived a very happy life.

Not far away from the couple's place, lived seven brothers of the king. They left for a walk into the forest and saw a beautiful girl and a dzo. They asked, "What are you doing? Where do you come from?" The girl said, "I am the princess of the southern kingdom. I came to look for this dzo." They said, "We brothers have no wife. Will you be our wife?" She replied, "Yes, I will" and they were married. The girl was really a demon and had come to kill them. There was a male demon too, he was disguised as the dzo. Each year, the demons killed one of the brothers, starting with the eldest. Then finally, it was the turn of the youngest brother to die. The ministers discussed this problem and said, "The rituals did not do any good for the elder brothers and they all died. To find an effective remedy, we must consult the pig-head diviner, who is gifted with a strong clairvoyance. As he lives behind two mountain passes, we must send for him immediately." They sent four horsemen out to get him. The four horsemen arrived at the diviner's house and conveyed the invitation. The husband said, "I am in retreat. I'll conduct the divination tonight and let you know of its outcome tomorrow." That night, he told this to his wife. She said, "So you must go to the palace, but it would be better to find a way to escape."

The next morning, the husband went to the horsemen and said, "The outcome from last night's divination was nice. Let us leave today." He put on his black costume, cropped his hair, carried a long rosary in his left hand and the pig's head with five colors of silk was held in his right hand and he mounted his horse. When they reached the king's palace, the devil couple was frightened as they saw his costume. Then he made a life-size ritual cake near the king's pillow. Stuck the pig's head on the top and then recited mantras.[3] The female demon freed the souls of the king. She had some doubt and sat thinking on the doorstep. The pain the king endured subsided and finally stopped. And, the king slept peacefully. The pig-head diviner was frightened. He wondered why the king, then writhing in agonizing pain, was now silent. He wondered if the king had died. Suddenly, he called out, "Oh king! Oh king!" There was no reply. Fearing that the king had died, he decided to flee. He took out the pig's head from the ritual cake and escaped.

As the husband entered a door, it happened to be the treasury. People shouted, "Thief! Thief! Hit him!" He again escaped and entered a kitchen. People again shouted, "Thief! Thief! Hit him!" Then he ran again, but found it impossible to escape. He entered into an enclosure, wondering who could be there. He saw a dzo, right beneath him. He at once hit it with the pig's head seven times between the horns and the dzo swiftly ran inside the place where the queen lived. The husband went there and eavesdropped. The male demon said, "The diviner has recognized me. He hit me seven times with his horrible staff. Now what do I do?" The queen said, "I am afraid that he may recognize me as well. So, I did not go near him. This noon every man in the kingdom was asked to come armed with weapons and every woman with firewood. He will first summon you and make you change from a dzo into your real form as a demon, which you cannot refuse. They will shoot arrows and spears and set you on a funeral pyre. Then he will order me to come and he will do the same thing."

As he overheard the conversation, the pig-head diviner thought that it will not be difficult now. Once again, he carried the pig's head and placed it on the ritual cake. Then he said to the king, "How is your health?" "After you came, my pain subsided and I slept well," said the king. The pig-head diviner then said, "Now please order your ministers to proclaim that every man in your kingdom come fully armed and every woman bring a load of wood tomorrow." This message was immediately sent out, he then set up a big funeral pyre at the center and lighted it on fire. The pig-head diviner said, "Saddle the dzo in the courtyard." He mounted the dzo and held the pig's head high and roamed around. Suddenly, he ordered, "Take off the saddle." Hitting the pig's head hard on the dzo, he shouted, "Change your form." The dzo at once turned into a horrifying demon with folds of flesh on his chest and blood oozing from his eyes. His upper fangs reached down to his chest, while his lower fangs touched up to his eyebrows. Terrified by the demon's looks, people attacked him with swords, spears, arrows and stones and finally killed him. Then people threw him into the hot funeral pyre. Then the pig-head diviner ordered, "Bring the queen here." She came crying, as people brought her along. The diviner wielded the pig's head high and said, "Change your form!" The queen changed her form into a female demon with breasts hanging low to her knees, long fangs and bloody eyes. People killed and burned her as well.

Then the pig-head diviner rode back to his palace. On the way, people bowed down to him on the road. Some cried out their respect, while some sprinkled grains or presented gifts to him. It took a whole day for him to reach back to the king's palace. The king was overjoyed when he returned to the palace and asked, "How should I reward you?" The husband said, "I want animal nose-rings, because we don't have many of them back home." The king loaded three sacks of nose-rings, meat, cheese and butter on seven elephants and he left for his home.

As the husband approached his village, his wife brought wine to welcome him. When she saw the loaded elephants, she said, "He is indeed the ideal man." They discussed everything in bed that night. She asked, "How did you uncover who the demons were?" The diviner narrated the entire story of how he subdued the demons and cured the king. She said, "You beggar! When you have everything before you, why ask only for animal nose-rings! You deserve more. Tomorrow, I am going to the palace."

The next day, his wife went to the palace with another forged letter that she wrote and she said to the king, "You had such a misfortune. You know it well. To get you rid of that misfortune, he has asked for just nose-rings. Now what my husband truly deserves is for your majesty to decide." Then she handed the king the forged letter. The king said, "That's true. This time I must invite the diviner and his family." When the diviner and his wife arrived at the palace. The king said, "It would not suffice to reward you separately. It is through your kindness that the demons are subdued and you saved my subjects and me from the demons. Let us rule the kingdom together. Your wife is wise, so let us both be her husband." This is what happened at the end.

Prince Gautamiputra remarked, "They're a fortunate couple." The Siddhivad corpse said, "The unfortunate prince talked. I will stay here no more" and the Siddhivad corpse flew away.

Here ends the fifteenth Siddhivad corpse story, The Diviner With the Pig-Head.

---

1. Tib. Bla g-yu, literally life-bearing turquoise, that determines the condition of one's life.
2. The dung cakes stuck on the walls can be stored for later use as fuel.
3. Almost every deity has a mantra. Oṃ Maṇi Padme Hūṃ is the mantra of Bodhisattva Avalokiteśvara and is the most popular mantra among Tibetans.

16 Two Brothers, Sūryaprabha and Candraprabha

Once again, Prince Gautamiputra walked the same route and arrived at Śītavana cemetery. He caught the Siddhivad corpse, carried the corpse on his back and began his journey back home. The corpse said, "The day is long and we are tired. Tell me an interesting story and I will listen. If you want me to tell you a story, just give a nod." The prince did not say a word.

The Siddhivad corpse then narrated the following story:

Long ago, there was a king named Samantabhāsa[1] who ruled over a very vast and beautiful kingdom. His queen gave birth to a prince, and they named him Sūryaprabha.[2] When his queen passed away, the king took another queen and they had another prince, who he named Candraprabha.[3] The new queen thought that her son, must become the king and not the older prince. Therefore, she plotted to kill prince Sūryaprabha.

One day, the queen pretended to be sick and wailed loudly as if writhing in unbearable pain. The king saw this and asked her, "Oh, my beautiful queen, what are you suffering from?" She said, "This is an illness I inherited from my parents, but this time it is very serious. There is a remedy, but it is difficult. There is no way for me but to die." The king said, "What is the remedy? If you die, it would break my heart. So, please tell me what I can do. I will do it even at the cost of my kingdom." The queen said, "The remedy lies in the hearts of either of the two princes. If I eat a prince's heart cooked in butter, I shall be cured. Nevertheless, I know the kingdom can not lose the future king, Sūryaprabha, and Candraprabha is my own son, so I cannot eat his heart. So, there is no way, I have to die." The king said, "I did not know that. It'd be unbearable, if you were to die. Tomorrow or the day after, I'll sacrifice Sūryaprabha for you. We can kill him and you can eat his heart." The king promised to do this. The younger prince Candraprabha overheard this conversation and went to his elder brother Prince Sūryaprabha. The younger brother said, "I heard father and mother are planning to kill you the day after tomorrow. What should we do now?" The elder brother said, "Be good and serve your mother well. Time has come for me to die." The younger brother Candraprabha became very sad and said, "If you are not here, I am not going to be here as well. I'll go wherever you go." They decided to do the same thing.

The next evening, as the full moon appeared, the two brothers left the palace. They did not arrange for any provisions, as they feared that the queen might learn about their flight. They took with them a bag of dry ritual cakes from a priest and headed east. They crossed many valleys and passes walking day and night. One day they came to a valley and found that they had run out of dry cakes and could not find any water. The younger brother collapsed on the ground and was speechless. The elder brother screamed, "Oh Brother, I'll go for water. Wait until I come back. Stay here and be courageous." The elder brother walked to the edge of a mountain but he could not find water. When he returned, his younger brother died due to thirst. The elder brother was very sad. He placed stones around Candraprabha's dead body and prayed that they meet again in their next life. The elder brother crossed two passes and came to a rocky mountain with a crevice that looked like a red door. He entered the cave and saw an old hermit. The hermit said, "Where did you come from?" The prince narrated his story in detail. The hermit said, "What a pity! Then be my son. I'll pray for the life of your brother." The hermit prayed to the Three Jewels[4] for help. As a result of the hermit's power of prayer and truth, the younger brother came to life, as if rising from a deep sleep. He traced the footprints of his elder brother and arrived at door of the hermit's house. The two brothers met each other and happily lived as the hermit's adopted sons.

The king of that kingdom was very successful and prosperous. In the upper valley of the kingdom was a lake inhabited by Nāgas. Whenever the farmers needed water to irrigate their fields, the king made offerings to the Nāgas. Every year the king sacrificed a boy born in the Year of the Tiger by drowning him in the lake. Many years later, there was no more tiger-year boys left. Around the secluded area where the hermit lived with his two sons, there were many animal herders. They saw the two boys living with the hermit. They asked, "Are you both the hermit's sons?" The two brothers replied, "Yes, we are." This is how, in time, the king came to know that the elder son, who lived with the hermit, was born in a tiger-year. The king immediately summoned four horsemen and ordered them, "Bring me the tiger-year boy." The four horsemen rode there and arrived at the door of the hermit. They said, "The king sent us here to take away your elder son." The hermit was very sad. He said, "How can an old man have sons?" Then he closed the door. He hid the boys in big jars and sealed them with clay as if they contained rice. The hermit sat on them wearing his long robe. Then the four horsemen said, "Search for the boy in the house." They broke the door open and checked the house. They searched all around, inside and outside, yet could not find them. They said, "If you do not give us your son, we will lose our job and our families." So they beat the hermit with heavy batons. Unable to bear the cries of the kind hermit, the sons shouted, "Please, don't beat our father, we are here." As they came out, the horsemen grabbed the elder brother Sūryaprabha and took him away. The hermit and the younger brother Candraprabha were deeply saddened.

Then as the elder brother Sūryaprabha arrived at the palace, the subjects reminded the king, "The date for drowning the tiger-year boy is today. So, please act fast." The king ordered this to be done. As they prepared to throw the elder brother into the lake, the princess of the kingdom said, "Please don't throw this boy into the lake." The king refused. Then the princess cried, "Then throw me into the lake with this boy." The king said, "My daughter is not concerned about my kingdom. Put the princess and the tiger-year boy in a leather sack and drown them together in the lake." "The king's order only needs to be said at once," said the subjects. They wrapped them in a leather bag, stitched the ends and drowned them in the lake for the Nāgas. When the elder brother in the bag was under the water, he became very sad and thought, "I was born in the year of the tiger and I fell victim to this sacrificial ritual. But why does this beautiful princess care for me so much? Why does she have to die with me? The princess thought differently, she thought, "I am a girl and I am dispensable for the king and his subjects. But how can they sacrifice such a handsome boy?" The Nāga was able to read her minds and did not kill them. Instead, they pushed them to the edge of the shore and they were saved. At the same time rain poured and the subjects were happy too. The Nāga told them that the kingdom need not sacrifice anybody in the future and that they would get rain all the time.

As the elder brother and the princess walked towards the kingdom, the elder brother said, "Oh princess, you must return to the palace. I'll go and see my hermit father and my younger brother at the place where they live." Having said this, they parted with the promise to marry each other, in this life. The princess returned to her palace.

The elder brother Sūryaprabha went to the area where his stepfather and younger brother lived. He knocked on the door and a meek voice asked, "Who are you?" He replied, "I am your son." The voice said, "Though I have two sons, the king took away and killed the elder one. We are stricken with sorrow." He reassured his father, "I am your son. I truly am. The king threw me into water, but the Nāgas did not eat me. Instead, they set me free. Father, don't be sad, please open the door." They said, "Sure, we will," and then walked towards the door. As they opened the door, the elder brother found them so weak and emaciated that they were almost dead. The elder brother Sūryaprabha bathed them in milk and water and calmed them with soothing words to alleviate their sorrows. This cheered their spirits.

When the princess returned to the palace, the king, his attendants and his subjects were all equally surprised. Everyone in the kingdom talked about her, "The king drowned people in the lake, where the vicious Nāga lived, but nobody returned alive and safe. This is indeed surprising!" Everyone walked around her and bowed low to her and honored her. The king said, "It's nice that my princess returned alive. What about that tiger-year boy?" She replied, "He is alive. Due to his kindness, the Nāga spared me. The Nāga is now subdued and demands no more tiger-year boys. The water will flow freely all the time now." The king said to his ministers, "That is amazing. Now, take me to the place where that boy lives." The ministers instead arranged for the boy from the upper valley, his brother and the hermit to come to the palace to see the king. As they approached the palace, the king extended a very warm welcome as a sign of gratitude for their kindness to come to him.

In the palace, the king seated them on thrones made of precious stones. The king asked, "You are an amazing boy. Are you truly the hermit's son?" The elder brother said, "I am the prince of a king. Since my stepmother plotted to kill me, I escaped and arrived at the hermit's area. The other boy is my younger brother..." Thus, he narrated his entire story. The king held him in high esteem. The king said, "Now, I am going to give my princess to you two brothers. I would also like to reward you with an inconceivable amount of wealth and will escort you back to your kingdom." With a vast amount of wealth and escorted by four groups of armed forces, they left for the brothers' kingdom.

When they were near their palace, they sent a messenger to inform King Samantabhāsa about their home-coming. King Samantabhāsa and his queen were depressed since the day the two brothers fled their land. As the king received the message, he was ecstatic and sent many people to receive them. The two brothers arrived at the palace with the princess and a lot of wealth. The cruel queen was shocked to see both brothers alive. Suddenly, she vomited blood and died.

Prince Gautamiputra said, "That's what she truly deserved." The corpse said, "The unfortunate prince spoke again. Now I will stay no more." Then, the Siddhivad corpse flew away.

Here ends the sixteenth Siddhivad corpse story, Tale of Two Brothers, Sūryaprabha and Candraprabha.

1. Tib. Kun snang (Skt. Samantabhāsa), literally means ever luminous.
2. Tib. Nyi ma'i 'od (Skt. Sūryaprabha), literally means rays of the sun.
3. Tib. Zla ba'i 'od (Skt. Candraprabha), literally means beam of the moon.
4. The Three Jewels (Tib. dkon mchog gsum, Skt. Triratna) comprises the teacher Buddha, his Dharma teachings and the Sangha community.

17 The Clever Man and the King

Once again, Prince Gautamiputra walked the same route and arrived at Śītavana cemetery. He caught the Siddhivad corpse, carried the corpse on his back and began his journey back home. The corpse said, "The day is long and we are tired. Tell me an interesting story and I will listen. If you want me to tell you a story, just give a nod." The prince did not say a word.

The Siddhivad corpse then narrated the following story:

Long ago, there was a kingdom called Śaligrama[1] where there lived a clever man named Mahānirmita.[2] The king of that kingdom was displeased with him and said, "You cannot stay in the kingdom, go somewhere else." As he was ordered, he left the kingdom.

One afternoon, the clever man arrived at a vast empty land overgrown with wild grass. As he reached the center of the land, he saw tall Tāla[3] trees and a dead horse. He cut the head for keepsake and carried it and climbed up one of the Tāla trees. When it turned dark, ghosts sporting wide hats and riding horses assembled below the tree. The ghosts were busy preparing various food and drinks. The clever man on the tree was extremely frightened, and accidentally dropped the horse head among the ghosts who were enjoying their feast. Some ghosts fainted, while others fled in all directions.

The next morning, the clever man checked out below what he saw that night. He thought, "There must be something here." Then he found a golden bowl filled with wine. He drank the wine and turned the bowl upside down, instantly it was filled with meat and food. He knew that it was a wish granting magical bowl and he took it with him. As the clever man walked further, he met a man carrying three amulets and a stick. He asked, "What is that stick for?" The man replied, "My stick is called, Whirling Stick. If you order it to take someone's belongings, the stick will kill the man and take the things from that person." He said, "I have a wish granting golden bowl. Then, would you like to exchange it for your stick?" The man said, "Yes I would like to." As the clever man got the stick in his hand, he said, "Oh, Whirling Stick, go and kill him. Then bring back the golden bowl." As soon as he uttered this, the stick soared into the air, killed the man and brought back the golden bowl.

Again as the clever man walked aimlessly down the road, he met a man with an iron hammer. He asked, "What does your iron hammer do?" The man replied, "If you hit the ground nine times with my hammer, you can have a nine-storey iron castle." The clever man said, "Then, would you like to exchange it for my wish granting golden bowl?" The man agreed and they exchanged the things. Again the clever man ordered his stick, "Oh, Whirling Stick, go and kill him. Then bring back the golden bowl." As soon as he uttered this, the stick soared into the air, killed the man and brought back the golden bowl.

The clever man walked further and met a man wearing a sheepskin. He asked, "What is this?" The man replied, "This is a magical skin. If you flap it mildly, it will bring a drizzle. If you flap it hard, it will produce heavy rain." He said, "Then, would you like to exchange it for my wish granting golden bowl?" The man agreed and they exchanged the things. Again the clever man ordered his stick, "Oh, Whirling Stick, go and kill him. Then bring back the golden bowl." As soon as he uttered this, the stick soared into the air, killed the man and brought back the golden bowl. The clever man then took all of the things with him and came back to his kingdom, thinking he will avenge the wicked king for his banishment. He went behind the palace and furiously hit the ground nine times with the iron hammer. Instantly there rose up a nine-storey iron castle.

The next day, the king learned about the new castle and said, "Yesterday, behind the palace, someone had built a nine-storey castle. That must be the work of the man named Mahānirmita.

Today, let's see who the winner is." The king ordered each of his subjects to bring a bag of charcoal and pile them around the iron castle. Then he asked all the iron-smiths to bring their bellows and blow fire on the fort." Thus, they lit a huge fire.

The clever man and his mother lived inside the iron fort. They ordered delicious food and drinks from the wish granting bowl and were safe. The mother, who lived on the eighth floor, saw half of her floor consumed by fire. The mother cried, "Son, our iron fort is in flames by the king's fire. Do something so that we will not be charred to death." He said to his mother, "Oh Mother, don't ever worry, I have a remedy for fire." He then flapped his magical sheepskin hard. Instantly, there fell heavy rain. It extinguished the fire around the iron fort and carried away the iron-smiths who blew the fire with the bellows. The son and the mother were safe and lived a happy life.

Prince Gautamiputra said, "That man named Mahānirmita had been more powerful than the king of the kingdom." The corpse said, "The unfortunate prince talked, I will not stay" and the Siddhivad corpse flew away.

Here ends the seventeenth Siddhivad corpse story, The Clever Man and the King.

---

1. Tib. 'Bras yul (Skt. Śāligrama), means the land of rice.
2. Tib. Dran gsal (Skt. Mahānirmita), means clever, skillful or intelligent one.
3. Tib. Ta la (Skt. Tāla) is a Sanskritised Tibetan name for Palmyra tree. (Bot. Borassus Flabelliformis)

18 The Bird-Skin King

Once again, Prince Gautamiputra walked the same route and arrived at Śītavana cemetery. He caught the Siddhivad corpse, carried the corpse on his back and began his journey back home. The corpse said, "The day is long and we are tired. Tell me an interesting story and I will listen. If you want me to tell you a story, just give a nod." The prince did not say a word.

The Siddhivad corpse then narrated the following story:

Once upon a time, in the kingdom of Udhyāna,[1] there lived a house owner with three daughters. Everyday, each daughter took turns to graze the buffaloes.

One day, it was the eldest daughter's turn to graze the buffaloes. She fell asleep and lost one buffalo. She went everywhere to search for it and finally found herself in front of a red door between two walls. She opened the door and walked inside. Then there was a turquoise door. She opened it and walked further. There was a nice and comfortable house filled with articles made of gold, turquoise, etc. There was nobody in the room, except for a white bird that perched on a seat made of precious jewels. She asked the bird, "I lost one of my buffaloes and can't find it. Have you seen my buffalo?" The bird said, "If you marry me, I'll tell you everything, if not, then I won't tell you anything." She replied, "I am not interested in living a worldly married life. Above all, you are an animal. Even if I can't find my buffalo, I don't mind, because I don't want to be your wife." Then she returned home.

The next day, the middle daughter went to graze the buffaloes. The same thing happened to her, she lost a buffalo and she met the white bird, as did her elder sister. The next day after that the youngest daughter went to graze the buffaloes. The same event occurred to her as to her two elder sisters. The white bird said, "If you marry me, I'll tell you where the buffalo is." The youngest daughter said, "Men, generally, speak the truth. As you are a male bird, you must be truthful too. So I'll marry you." She then became his wife.

Once, there was a carnival at a temple, which lasted for thirteen days. The youngest daughter also went to see the carnival. She found herself amidst a big gathering where she happened to be the most beautiful woman. The most handsome man in the crowd was there and rode a blue horse. He circled her three times and rode away. She overheard people saying to one another, "He is the best man." When the youngest daughter returned home, the white bird asked, "Who was the best man and the best woman in today's gathering?" She replied, "The handsomest man was riding a blue horse. I do not know who he is. I seem to have been the most beautiful woman that was there." The same thing happened for eleven days. On the twelfth day, as the youngest daughter returned from the market, she stayed in the house of her neighbor, an old woman. The old woman asked, "Who was the best man and woman in today's gathering?" She replied, "The handsomest man was riding a blue horse. I don't know who he is. I seem to have been the most beautiful woman there. What a pity! If I could get this handsome rider of the blue horse, I would not want anything else. Unfortunately, my husband is an animal." Then, she cried. The old woman said, "Girl, don't say this. You may be the most beautiful woman, but listen to me, the man riding the blue horse is your husband. Tomorrow is the thirteenth day of the gathering. Just pretend to be leaving your home for the carnival, but hide behind the door. Soon he will shed his bird's skin and leave. He will leave for the carnival riding on a blue horse. Then you should burn his bird skin and you will see his human body forever." The youngest daughter did this the next day.

The youngest daughter burned the bird skin in a fire and waited at the fireplace for her husband to return. As the sun was setting, he came home and said, "You have arrived earlier than me." She said, "Yes." He asked, "Where is my bird skin?" She said, "I burned it." He said, "Alas! You have committed a grave mistake, as that was my true soul." She regretted what she had done and said, "What can I do now?" He said, "There is no other way but to keep watch at the door and wag a stick day and night for a week. If you stop, ghosts will take me away and I will have to fight with the ghosts." Then the youngest daughter took a stick, fixed a straw grass blade between her upper and lower eyelids to avoid sleeping. She wagged the stick for six days, but felt asleep for a moment. The ghosts took her husband away saying, "Here we take the bird skin king."

The youngest daughter became very sad and roamed alone in the wilderness, searching everywhere. In a painful and melodic voice, she called out, "Where are you, my bird skin king?" She searched day and night, but could not find any trace of him. One day, the youngest daughter heard his voice. It was a high pitched voice, though it was a sad voice. She heard that voice coming from the ground underneath her feet. As she followed the voice, she met the bird skin king near a mountain pass carrying a load of shoes. He said, "Glad to see you again. I have to fetch water for the ghosts as long as these shoes last. Do not come after me. Instead, go home and make a new bird skin and conduct the proper rituals to restore my life. Maybe I can come to life again." Then suddenly, he was a ghost that was carried away like the wind. She then made a new bird skin and performed the restoration rituals. Instantly, the bird skin king escaped from the ghost land and arrived at her door.

Prince Gautamiputra said, "How happy she must have been!" The Siddhivad corpse flew away saying, "The unfortunate prince finally spoke. I will not stay here any more."

Here ends the eighteenth Siddhivad corpse story, The Bird-Skin King.

---

1. Tib. skyed mos tshal (Skt. Udhyāna) means garden or garden-like.

19 Painter Ānanda and Carpenter Ānanda

Once again, Prince Gautamiputra walked the same route and arrived at Śītavana cemetery. He caught the Siddhivad corpse, carried the corpse on his back and began his journey back home. The corpse said, "The day is long and we are tired. Tell me an interesting story and I will listen. If you want me to tell you a story, just give a nod." The prince did not say a word.

The Siddhivad corpse then narrated the following story:

Once upon a time, there lived a king named Samantabhāsa[1] who ruled over a vast kingdom called Sarvapraṇidhana.[2] When the king died, his son, Prince Sarvāpāla,[3] succeeded as king and ruled the kingdom. Among his subjects were two persons that had the same name of Ānanda.[4] One was a painter and the other was a carpenter. These two men hated each other.

Once, the painter Ānanda went to King Sarvāpāla. He said, "Last night, I went to see your father, who is now in heaven. He has accumulated an inconceivable amount of wealth and power. This is a letter from your father." The painter Ānanda handed the letter to King Sarvāpāla. The letter read: "My dear son Sarvāpāla, after I died, I was reborn in heaven among the gods and I have a lot of wealth. As I am planning to build a temple, I cannot find carpenters up here. Could you send me your carpenter Ānanda? I have instructed the painter Ānanda on how the carpenter, Ānanda should travel to heaven." Then, he handed the forged letter to the king.

After King Sarvāpāla read his father's letter, he said, "I must do what my father wants. Bring the carpenter Ānanda here." As the carpenter appeared, King Sarvāpāla said, "My father is in heaven. He wants you to go there to build a temple. Here is my father's letter." Merely looking at the letter, the carpenter Ānanda knew that it was a plot by the painter Ānanda. Then he asked, "Oh King, I shall do as you say, but how do I go to heaven?" The king replied, "For this, we must ask the painter Ānanda." So, he was summoned. The painter Ānanda explained, "There is a way to reach heaven. You must carry all your tools and sit on a funeral pyre of wood drenched in oil. As we light the pyre, accompanied by loud music, you shall ride the smoke like a horse and go to heaven." The carpenter said, "I'll do what you say. But I prefer going to heaven from the field behind my house." They decided he was to go after seven days. The carpenter Ānanda returned home and said to his wife, "The painter Ānanda has plotted to kill me. But I will do things my way." He and his wife dug a tunnel from under their house to the center of the field. They covered the opening with slates and mud.

After seven days, King Sarvāpāla declared, "Today carpenter Ānanda will go to my father's palace. All subjects should each bring wood and a pint of oil to the field." The king arranged for everything accordingly and built a huge funeral pyre in the middle of the carpenter's field. Then they placed the carpenter with his tools in the center. They lit the wood that was around him and played loud music. A big fire burned making heavy smoke. The carpenter Ānanda took all his tools with him and went home through the secret tunnel. Painter Ānanda was very happy. He pointed towards the sky, he shouted, "Look, the carpenter Ānanda is going to heaven on a smoke horse." Then the gathering dispersed. Every one talked about it saying, "The carpenter Ānanda left to be with our late king in heaven."

The carpenter Ānanda hid in his home for one month and kept away from everybody. He washed himself every day with milk. Then he put on a while silk cloth, prepared a forged letter addressed to King Sarvāpāla and went to the palace. The letter read, "Dear son Sarvāpāla, it is nice that you are in good health and rule the kingdom according to the Dharma. Here the carpenter Ānanda has served me very well. The wooden buildings

are all completed. He should get a huge gift and a grand feast. Now, the temple needs painting, it is important that we immediately sent the painter Ānanda. He can follow the same route as the carpenter." The carpenter Ānanda took the letter to King Sarvāpāla. When the king saw carpenter Ānanda, the king asked, "It is good that you returned from heaven. Is my father well and happy?" As a reply, the carpenter Ānanda handed the forged letter to the king. King Sarvāpāla read it and said, "You are right." The king rewarded him with many gifts. Then king Sarvāpāla ordered, "My late father needs a painter for the newly constructed temple. Now, bring painter Ānanda here." When the painter Ānanda arrived, the king gave him the letter. Painter Ānanda also saw that carpenter Ānanda had a light skin fair complexion and he was dressed in white silk and wore many ornaments. He was surprised to see him alive and wondered how he returned. The painter Ānanda believed the letter to be true and thought that the king's late father must be waiting for him. The painter Ānanda also thought that the carpenter must have really gone to heaven by riding the smoke, as he himself saw the fire consume the carpenter. It was also too late to refuse to go.

The painter agreed to go to heaven after seven days and asked, "How should I go?" The king said, "You should follow the same method as the carpenter." On the seventh day, all the king's subjects collected wood and oil and they prepared another funeral pyre in the middle of a field. They placed painter Ānanda in the middle of the wood. He held all his painting materials, offerings for the late King Samantabhāsa and a letter from King Sarvāpāla in his hand. They lit the pyre from different directions. All around the pyre, people played loud music. The painter cried out in pain and tried to jump out, but his voice was inaudible amidst the loud music and the disturbance going on. In this way, he was burned to ash.

Prince Gautamiputra said, "He asked for it. He got the results from his own doing." The corpse said, "The unfortunate prince finally spoke. Now I will not stay here." The Siddhivad corpse flew away.

Here ends the nineteenth Siddhivad corpse story, Painter Ānanda and Carpenter Ānanda.

1. Tib. Kun snang (Skt. Samantabhāsa), means ever-luminous.
2. Tib. Kun smon (Skt. Sarvapraṇidhana), rendered as in Tibetan, means ever-inspiring.
3. Tib. Kun skyong (Skt. Sarvāpāla), means ever-caring.
4. Tib. Kun dga' (Skt. Ānanda), literally means ever-joyous or liked by all.

20 The Girl Who Retrieved a Lost Heart

Once again, Prince Gautamiputra walked the same route and arrived at Śītavana cemetery. He caught the Siddhivad corpse, carried the corpse on his back and began his journey back home. The corpse said, "The day is long and we are tired. Tell me an interesting story and I will listen. If you want me to tell you a story, just give a nod." The prince did not say a word.

The Siddhivad corpse then narrated the following story:

Long ago, a king named Vairocana,[1] ruled over a vast kingdom called, Puṇḍravardhana.[2] The king passed away and his very handsome, strong and clever prince was enthroned as king. The new king took the princess of a southern kingdom as his queen, but he did not love the queen. About a Yojana[3] further from the border of his kingdom, there lived a very beautiful girl. The king loved her and always went to see her. After a while, the king fell ill and died. The girl was carrying his child and did not get the news of the king's death.

One night, when the moon was bright, the girl heard a knock at her door. When the girl opened the door, she saw the king, he was completely naked and without ornaments. Extremely overjoyed, she held his hands and invited him into her house and she served him rice wine. The king got up and asked her to follow him. As she walked, he beckoned, "Come further down this way." Again, she followed him and finally they arrived near the palace. As the girl heard music coming from inside the palace, she asked, "What is this?" The king said, "You don't seem to know. They're observing the seventh-day ritual as a part of my post-funeral rites."[4] She wondered why it was a funeral rite. Then the king explained, "I am dead. As you are carrying my child, make sure that the child is born in the elephant barn. Inside the palace, my mother and queen are quarreling about my turquoise gem, which I have hidden under my mattress. Give that turquoise gem to my queen and send her back to her home. My mother and you should take care of the kingdom until my son grows up." Then he vanished in thin air. She was extremely sad and cried, "Oh my king! Oh my king!" Then she could feel the first surge of her labor pains and went into the elephant barn. That night, she gave birth to a son.

The next morning at day-break, the elephant keeper (a mahout) came to the elephant barn. He shouted, "Oh! A woman had delivered a child in the elephant barn. This might pollute the royal elephants." The girl heard it and said, "Please, call the late king's mother and ask her to come here." The king's mother came and the girl told her everything. The king's mother said, "It is wonderful to have an heir, now let us go to the palace." The king's mother loved the boy very dearly. The king's mother also found the turquoise gem that the girl told her about, so the king's mother was convinced about the truth of her story. The king's mother gave the turquoise gem to the queen and sent her back to her kingdom. Together, the king's mother and the girl ruled the kingdom.

Then every month, on the full moon, the king visited the boy at night and spent the whole night with him, but left the boy at dawn. The girl recounted these visits to the king's mother. The king's mother said, "It can't be true, if it is, just hold him back for a short time after dawn, so I can see him too." The girl did this and let the king's mother take a quick look at the late king. She recognized him and then asked the girl, "Could you set a meeting between the two of us? I am his mother and I want to see my only son."

Then one full moon night, when the king came back, the girl told him, "It is good to see you every full moon night, but it pains me to think of why we can't stay together forever." Then she wept. The king said, "If you have courage, you can make me come to

life again and we can live together forever. However, as women are less courageous, it is too difficult a thing for you to accomplish." The girl said, "If I could live with you in this life, I assure you that even if my flesh and bones are torn apart, I will strive to do it." The king said, "The next full moon night as the moon waxes completely, walk one Yojana towards the south and you will see an old iron man drinking molten iron, he will be saying, "I am very thirsty." You have to give him a bag of rice wine. Then as you go on, there will be two sheep fighting with each other. Give them some beer sediment.[5] Then going further, there will be people wielding weapons against one another. Give them some meat to eat. If you go on, next there will be a terrifying black house. The floors of the house will be covered in blood and it has banners of human skin hanging everywhere. At the door of that house, there will be two Yamas[6] with there hair in thick locks. Give them blood offerings. Then as you enter the house, there will be a Maṇḍala surrounded by eight scary tantric priests. Around the Maṇḍala, there are nine hearts. Eight of the old hearts will plead, "Please take us," while a fresh looking heart will cry, "Please, don't take me." Without any fear and hesitation, grab that heart and bring it here. Walk straight back to me and never turn back to look. If you can bring the new heart here, I will be revived and we can have a whole life-time together."

With all of this on her mind, the girl on the next full moon night left towards the south without anyone seeing her. One by one, she gave all the gifts away and arrived at the black house. She stealthily entered the house and quickly took the new heart and fled. The tantric priests followed her and shouted at the two Yama gatekeepers, "She stole our heart, catch her!" They let her go saying, "Let her go, she gave us blood offerings." The tantric priests then shouted at the men, "Catch her!" They said, "She gave us food" and they too let her go. Again, the tantric priests shouted at the two sheep, "Catch the thief," but they refused saying, "She gave us beer sediment" and they let her go. So, the tantric priests asked the old iron man, "Catch that thief, she stole our heart," but he said, "She gave me rice wine." In the end, everyone let her go.

The girl ran fast and she arrived back at the palace. She opened the gate and entered the palace and saw her husband there wearing many ornaments. She was very happy and they embraced.

Prince Gautamiputra said, "That was a great woman." The corpse said, "The unfortunate prince finally spoke. Now I will stay here no more." Then, the Siddhivad corpse flew away.

Here ends the twentieth Siddhivad corpse story, The Girl Who Retrieved a Lost Heart.[7]

---

1. Tib. Snang mdzad pa can (Skt. Vairocana), means ever-luminous.
2. Tib. Bu ram 'phel (Skt. Puṇḍravardhana), means producing sugarcane.
3. An ancient Indic unit of length, approximately equal to a mile or a league.
4. Post-funerary rites conducted weekly for seven times to ensure the deceased a higher rebirth and liberation in his or her future lives.
5. Leftover waste of the fermented grain, after beer has been brewed.
6. Tib. Gshin rje (Skt. Yama) is generic name for the King of Death or his messengers in Indic religions.
7. The theme, plot and characters are similar to story 11 in this book, The Girl Who Retrieved the King's Spirit from Death.

21 The Couple

Once again, Prince Gautamiputra walked the same route and arrived at Śītavana cemetery. He caught the Siddhivad corpse, carried the corpse on his back and began his journey back home. The corpse said, "The day is long and we are tired. Tell me an interesting story and I will listen. If you want me to tell you a story, just give a nod." The prince did not say a word.

The Siddhivad corpse then narrated the following story:

Long ago, there lived two brothers in the kingdom called Kṣīrajanpada.[1] The elder brother took a wife for himself to continue his ancestry lineage. Then he expelled his younger brother from his house because he was jealous of him.

As the days passed, the elder brother became very rich and wealthy and wanted to host a grand feast for the village. The younger brother thought, "My brother doesn't intend to do anything good for me, but at least he will invite me to the village feast." As the first day of the feast passed, the younger brother was left out and not invited. Then on the second day, he thought, "I was not invited yesterday. Maybe because today is really the actual day of the feast, surely my elder brother will invite me." However, he was not invited. The younger brother hoped that his elder brother would invite him the next day, which was the final day of the feast. Even then, he was not invited. So he became very sad. Then the younger brother thought, "Tonight, everyone will be drunk. I must steal the most precious thing from my elder brother's house. He entered his house and hid himself among some things in a room. People were drunk before the sun went down and they all went to bed early.

The younger brother saw his elder brother's wife bring her drunken husband back to the bedroom and put him to sleep.

The wife pretended to sleep with him as he fell asleep. Then she got up and filled a utensil with food, meat, butter, garlic, onions and other food. She also took some barley and rice wine with her. Then the elder brother's wife left the house. Completely taken by surprise, the younger brother canceled his plans to steal something from the house and instead followed her.

The wife climbed a high mountain and reached a horrible cemetery that was behind the house. The younger brother also climbed up and arrived there. The wife walked into the middle of a green meadow and went up to a grave covered with a white slab. The wife went there to meet a white corpse. It was once her lover whose spirit remained behind to be with her even after his death. Dead bodies like this were not eaten by wild beasts and birds in cemeteries. She called out his name from a distance when she saw the corpse and ran towards him and she embraced him. She put some food in her mouth then and pushed it into the corpse's mouth using her tongue. As she did this, the stick that was keeping the corpse's mouth open, snapped and cut the tip of her nose. The tip of her tongue was also cut and a piece of it remained in the corpse's mouth. There was a lot of bleeding and she sadly returned home taking the utensils with her.

The younger brother also managed to arrive back before her and hid again in her room. Then as she got back into her bed, her husband woke up from his sleep. Immediately, she cried, "You are such a bad husband. You must listen to what others say: Why did you cut my nose and my tongue?" The husband replied, "I did not cut your tongue." The wife said, "I know what you did. Tomorrow, I am going to report this to the king." As they argued with each other, the younger brother left the room without stealing anything.

The next morning, the wife went to the king's palace and cried, "Oh king! Last night, my husband behaved badly, beyond my expectations. Please, punish him correctly." The king summoned the elder brother and made them discuss it in public. The wife told many things that all sounded very true. However, the elder brother could only say, that he remembered nothing.

The king said, "The husband can't be truthful" and ordered that the husband be tied to the death pole. When the elder brother was about to die, the younger brother heard what was happening to his brother. The younger brother went to see him and asked, "What wrong have you done?" The elder brother explained everything to his younger brother.

The younger brother requested to see the king and told him, "Oh your majesty, you must know the truth. You cannot do anything without examining things first. Now, please call my brother and his wife here. I'll tell you everything, your majesty." The king then summoned the couple to the palace. The younger brother told everything in detail, including the wife's visit to the cemetery. The younger brother said, "If your highness is not convinced, please send someone to check if the tip of her tongue is still in the corpse's mouth. You will also find the broken piece of spoon and blood that bled from her nose there too."

The king immediately sent guards to investigate what was in the cemetery and found exactly what the younger brother told about in his story. The king said, "What the husband said is in fact true." The lying set the elder brother free[2] and tied the wife to the death pole and killed her.

The Prince Gautamiputra remarked, "The elder brother's wife got what she truly deserved, a befitting reward!" The corpse said, "Oh! The unfortunate prince spoke. Now I shall stay here no more." Then, the Siddhivad corpse flew away.

Here ends the twenty-first Siddhivad corpse story, The Couple.

---

1. Tib. 'O ma'i ljongs (Skt. Kṣīrajanpada), literally means land of milk.
2. The Tibetan version states that the king brought him down from the top of the pole but the actual scene indicates that they both are on the ground in front of the king and arguing. Therefore, I have translated that the man was set free.

22 Lady Hemapradīp

Once again, Prince Gautamiputra walked the same route and arrived at Śītavana cemetery. He caught the Siddhivad corpse, carried the corpse on his back and began his journey back home. The corpse said, "The day is long and we are tired. Tell me an interesting story and I will listen. If you want me to tell you a story, just give a nod." The prince did not say a word.

The Siddhivad corpse then narrated the following story:

Long ago, in the middle of a narrow valley, there was a place where people who were passing from either direction stayed for a night. There was an old temple that had a tall Avalokiteśvara[1] statue that was one-storey high.

Once, a poor man who was from the lower valley arrived there from the upper valley. He was carrying a large wooden box of fruit. Adjacent to the temple there was a small house where an old couple and their daughter lived. The poor man decided to eavesdrop and he heard a conversation the old couple were having from the roof opening of their small house. The old mother said, "We are growing old. Our daughter Hemapradīp[2] should be given for marriage." The old father said, "Our wealth, our comfortable life, our turquoise gems and everything, including our daughter, are due to our prayers and faith to the statue of Avalokiteśvara. Tomorrow on the eighth day, we will make offerings to Avalokiteśvara. We will then consult the statue on whether Hemapradīp should pursue religion or lead a married life and who she should marry. This will provide us with advice about what to do." The poor man overheard this, he thought that he must do something to win their daughter's hand. That night he opened the door of the temple, carved out a space in the back of the Avalokiteśvara statue and hid himself in it.

Early in the morning, the old couple and their daughter came into the temple, gave offerings and bowed down in respect. The old father implored, "Should our daughter pursue the Dharma or must she lead a secular life? If she were to marry, who do we choose as her soul mate? Please tell us now or you may appear later in our dreams tonight." The poor man placed his mouth behind the nose of Avalokiteśvara and pretended to be speaking as Avalokiteśvara. He said, "Your daughter should be married. Give her to whoever first comes to your door tomorrow. All your plans for your daughter will be instantly accomplished." The old couple said, "Avalokiteśvara has finally spoken." Deeply satisfied, they bowed down again many times to the statue and returned home. The poor man also came out from the back of the Avalokiteśvara statue.

The next morning, when it was very early, he went to their house and knocked the door. The old mother came out and saw him. She at once went back and said, "The man prophesied by Avalokiteśvara has come." The old father asked her, "Invite him in the house at once." He came into the house and they served him delicious food and drinks. They also offered him their daughter, a pint size box of turquoise gems and told him everything that happened the day before. The poor man said, "I shall do whatever you ask of me." He took the box of turquoise gems and left with the girl.

When the poor man was near his village in the lower valley, he reflected on how he deceived the old couple and took their daughter with him the previous day. He put the girl and turquoise gems in the wooden fruit box and buried them under the sand. Then he went to his village and told the people, "In the past, I tried every way to grow rich, but to no avail. This time, I will conduct an exorcism to chase away the hungry spirits." He took the ingredients and performed the ritual. The next day he arranged to do another ritual with other ingredients. He said, "Today, I must perform a fortune harvesting ritual." He then conducted that ritual.

Meanwhile, a prince from a neighboring kingdom arrived near the village and was in the desert, where Hemapradīp lay buried. Armed with a bow and arrows, the prince was followed by his pet tiger and three attendants. The prince said, "Let me shoot an arrow at that mound of black sand." Thus he shot the arrow and it struck the wooden box under the sand. As the prince opened the box, he found the girl and the turquoise gems. The prince asked, "Who are you?" She said, "I am a Nāga's daughter." He said, "If you agree to be my queen, I can rescue you." She said, "I can't go, I belong here in this box." However, the prince took the girl and the turquoise gems out and placed his tiger in the wooden box.

Back in the village, the poor man thought, "After completing my fortune harvesting ritual, I'll reveal to the people the girl and the turquoise gems and I will be a rich man." He returned to the desert to get the girl. He unearthed the box and carried it back to his home. He kept the box near the window in his attic. He said to his family, "I have to perform an additional quick fortune harvesting ritual. You may hear loud noises, but no one must come to my room." He locked the door and windows of his attic, so that the girl could not escape. Having changed into his bedclothes and when he felt relaxed, he opened the box. Instantly, the tiger sprang out at him. Out of fear, he shouted, "Help! Tiger! Tiger is here, boy, girl, help me!" With all his clothes torn to shreds, he cried and struggled with the tiger. His son and daughter laughed and said, "Our father's quick fortune harvesting ritual is a very noisy one." The next morning, as they entered their father's room they saw a big tiger in a corner of the room. The tiger's mouth and paws were bloodstained. The tiger had eaten their father, except for a few pieces of his bones.

The girl became the queen. She gave birth to three princes and lived a happy life. One day, the subjects gossiped among themselves, "Our king is not wise. He made a girl unearthed from the desert as his queen. It is not nice for the king's sons not to have any maternal uncles." The queen heard this and was sad. She thought, "Although I have three sons, what the people are talking about doesn't sound nice. I must go and see my old parents."

On a full moon night, the queen left the palace. The next day, as the sun rose, she arrived near to her parents' place. There were many fields she had not seen before and many farmers plowing the fields. Among them was a dark complexioned man wearing nice ornaments. He asked her, "Where did you come from?" She replied, "From a distant land." He asked, "Where are you going?" She replied, "My old parents live behind this mountain. I am going to check if they are doing fine." Then he asked, "Are you their daughter?" "Yes, I am," she replied. He said, "Yesterday a man, who claimed to be the old couple's son, came here. He said that he had a sister. I think it must be you. I will introduce him to you. Sit and have some food and drinks." He introduced her to the young man who claimed to be her brother and they decided to walk to her parent's house. As she looked from the edge of the mountain, she was surprised to see that in place of her old house, there stood a magnificent mansion. It was larger than a palace and decorated with victory flags, banners and bells. The Avalokiteśvara temple now looked bigger and better. It was decorated with a golden tower, banners, and bells. She asked, "Who owns these buildings?" He replied, "These are all ours, which I built. Our parents are well." As she entered the place, she could see signs of wealth and prosperity everywhere, there were many horses and mules in stables. Her parents now sat on silk cushions. As they saw their daughter, they asked, "Are you all fine? We are alive and it is nice that you have come to see us." Then she recounted all that had happened to her. The parents said, "The king and the ministers have told us the same story." They invited the king with his attendants and served them well for three days. The king and all the guests were very impressed and said, "The queen has parents and what the people gossiped about was not true." Then the king and the ministers left satisfied, but the queen extended her stay by another day, as she could not immediately leave her parents. She stayed behind, talked with them more until she was satisfied.

The next morning, she felt her pillow had turned hard. She wondered, "Why is this so hard? Am I not sleeping in my parent's house on a silk mattress?" As she looked around, she was very upset to find that their old hut was in ruins. Her parents died long before and their bones were scattered near the door. She found herself lying on the bare ground with only a white stone slab as her pillow. She became very sad. She came out to see the temple. It was also in ruins and the Avalokiteśvara statue was damaged. Then she thought, "Maybe Avalokiteśvara might have appeared to her in the form of hėr parents. Now, I must go to the king."

When she was nearly back home to her palace, the subjects saw the queen coming and they said, "This queen has great parents and she has given birth to handsome princes too. She is beautiful and possesses inconceivable qualities." They made elaborate arrangements and welcomed her back to the palace.

Prince Gautamiputra remarked, "What a lucky girl!" Immediately, the corpse said, "Oh unfortunate prince, you finally spoke. Now, I'll stay here no more." Then, the Siddhivad corpse flew away.

Here ends the twenty-second Siddhivad corpse story, Lady Hemapradīp.

1. Tib. Spyan ras gzigs (Skt. Avalokiteśvara) He is the embodiment of compassion of all Buddhas and disciple of Buddha Amitābha. Tibetans believe that Tibet is the chosen land of Avalokiteśvara and the Dalai Lama, one of its many emanations.
2. Tib. gser sgron ma (Skt. Hemapradīpa) literally means golden lamp.

23 The Clever Man

Once again, Prince Gautamiputra walked the same route and arrived at Śītavana cemetery. He caught the Siddhivad corpse, carried the corpse on his back and began the journey home. The corpse said, "The day is long and we are tired. Tell me an interesting story and I will listen. If you want me to tell you a story, just give a nod." The prince did not say a word.

The Siddhivad corpse then narrated the following story:

Once upon a time, there was a great kingdom called Puṣpamaṇḍīta.[1] It was a very pleasant place with sandalwood and mango trees and grapes and other fruit trees scattered all around. It had rich fields of various crops and gentle rivers. In the middle of the kingdom stood a magnificent palace called Tuṣita,[2] surrounded by many towns. That kingdom was ruled by a king named Bālabuddhi.[3]

Once, King Bālabuddhi addressed one of his subjects named Sphuṭabuddhi,[4] "If you are the one called Sphuṭabuddhi, you should be able to steal my life turquoise gem. If you can steal it, you will be highly rewarded. But should you fail to steal it, I'll take away your land and your eyes too." "Please, don't push me into doing this," requested the man, but the king refused. Therefore, he promised to steal it on the night of the next full moon. The king tied his life turquoise gem securely around his neck and decided never to go outside. He deployed men to guard everywhere in his palace.

Then on the night of the 15th day, the man carried a pitcher of strong rice wine and left his home. He gave the wine to the horse mounted guards at the palace gate. To the guards, the man said, "I know, I can't get the life turquoise gem, but the king refused to consider my objections about sealing it." He gave them more wine and then he went away. The guards drank more and more until they became unconscious. At midnight, the man reappeared at the palace gate carrying a half dried stomach of an animal, a straw hat and three pebbles from the river. At the gate, the guards were drunk and the horses were asleep. He could easily take the guards off their horses and put them on the pavement wall. Then he entered the palace. In the kitchen, two maids were sleeping in their clothes, so that they could make fire as soon as they woke up. He put the straw hat on the head of the maid that was closest to the fireplace. Then he slipped the three pebbles into the sleeve of the other maid sitting next to her and tied the maids together with a string.

Then the man left the kitchen to search for the life turquoise gem in the king's bedroom. The king was fast asleep and he saw the dazzling life turquoise gem around his neck. He covered the king's head with the half dried stomach of the animal. There were guards but they were sleeping with their heads resting together. He tied the braids of their hair to each other. Then, he removed the life turquoise gem from the king's neck and fled downstairs stomping noisily. Everybody shouted, "Thief! Thief!" However, the guards with their braids tied to each other shouted, "Please hold on, do not pull that way" and they were trying to release the knots in their hair. The king shouted, "Come here! My life turquoise gem is stolen and my head has all dried up." In the kitchen, the maids heard this and they blew air into the fire. The straw hat on one of the maids caught fire and her hair caught fire too. The other maid tried to put out the fire using her hands, but the three rocks in her sleeve wounded the maid. As they were busy treating her wounds, they could not chase the thief.

The maids shouted to the guards at the gate, "Chase the thief!" They still were completely drunk, they only kept hitting the sides of the walls with their feet and remained in one place.

The next day, the man appeared before the king with the life turquoise gem. The king was very angry. The man said to the king, "Your majesty, please don't be offended. I'll return your

life turquoise gem to you." The king yelled, "Do whatever you like with it. You covered my head with a half dried stomach and now it has all dried up." The queen came out and shouted, "He is such a bad person. He should be taken to court and beheaded." The man thought, "Right now, the king is not going to do anything good." Infuriated, he hit the life turquoise hard on a rock. It caused the king to start to bleed from his nose and he immediately died.

Astonished, Prince Gautamiputra remarked, "How foolish was that king!" The corpse said, "The unfortunate prince finally spoke. Now I will stay here no more." Then the Siddhivad corpse flew away.

Here ends the twenty-third Siddhivad corpse story, The Clever Man.

---

1. Tib. Me tog gis brgyan pa (Skt. Puṣpamaṇḍīta), literally means decorated by flowers.
2. Tib. Dga' ldan (Skt. Tuṣita), meaning the joyous, is one of the many heavenly abodes in Buddhist cosmology.
3. Tib. Byis pa'i blo can (Skt. Bālabuddhi), means one with child's intelligence.
4. Tib. Gsal ba'i blo can (Skt. Sphuṭabuddhi), means clever minded.

24 The Brahman's Son

Once again, Prince Gautamiputra walked the same route and arrived at Śītavana cemetery. He caught the Siddhivad corpse, carried the corpse on his back and began his journey back home. The corpse said, "The day is long and we are tired. Tell me an interesting story and I will listen. If you want me to tell you a story, just give a nod." The prince did not say a word.

The Siddhivad corpse then narrated the following story:

Once upon a time, there lived a Brahman's[1] son in a remote land. At one time, he sold his field for three rolls of woolen cloth. He loaded them on a donkey and left for another place.

As the Brahman boy walked on, he came across a group of children who had caught a mouse. They tied a rope to its neck, dipped it in water and dragged the poor creature all around. He felt pity for the mouse and could not stand the mistreatment. He shouted at the children, "This is sinful! Please release this mouse." The children replied, "We wanted it, that is why we trapped it. You fool!" He said, "Then I'll buy it. What do you say?" He bought it for one roll of wool. They freed the mouse and it ran to the crevices of the stonewall.

As he went further down the road, he saw another group of children playing with a monkey at an intersection. Having caught the monkey, they forced it to imitate their acts. As the monkey could not do what they wanted, the children beat the monkey with sticks. Again, he boldly told the children, "Let the poor creature go," but they did not listen. He gave another roll of wool and the monkey was freed into the forest.

As he walked further towards the outskirts of the city, he saw a group of children teasing a bear that they had caught. They were riding on it and beating it mercilessly. He could not stand the sight, he gave the last roll of wool and freed the bear into the forest. The Brahman boy then had no more rolls of wool left.

While walking alongside his donkey, he thought that he had come to do business, but now there was nothing left and he felt helpless. He came to a palace and passed the guards at the gates and entered the palace. He then went to the treasure house in the palace yard. He took a load of silk and ran away. When he was near the gate, he saw the queen, she cried out, "Thief! Thief in the palace!" All the people gathered around and caught him. The king ordered, "Put this thief into a special wooden case, nail the case shut and throw it into the river." The attendants did what the king ordered and they threw him into the river.

The water carried the case away and finally landed on the shore of a small island. He was about to suffocate in the box, but after a short time, he heard a scratching sound from outside the box. A mouse made a small opening in the box and he saw that it was the same mouse that was saved earlier in exchange for a roll of wool. The mouse said, "Relax, I'll call your two friends," and he went away. The Brahman boy could finally breathe easy. The mouse went to the monkey and told the monkey everything that happened. The monkey came and broke most of the braces of the box. Then the bear arrived and tore the box into pieces. Then the three brought him fruit to eat. He ate the fruit and they all stayed together near the river. When night fell, they saw a bright light shining from the other side of the river. He sent the monkey to look and he came back with a wish granting jewel, almost the size of a duck's egg. As soon as the Brahman boy received it, he prayed, "May I safely reach the other side of the river." Instantly, he was already there. Again, he closed his eyes and prayed, "At the center of this piece of land, may there appear a magnificent house with a beautiful temple surrounded by fields of many different types of growing crops, such as rice, barley and many kinds of fruits, like nectar water springs, etc." He also wished, "May the house be filled with many expensive things." When he opened his eyes he saw everything he had wished for. He lived a very comfortable life.

Once, a wealthy merchant arrived at that place by the river. He was very surprised to see how it had changed and exclaimed, "Amazing! This was just an empty ground before, but now it has all changed." The merchant went to the Brahman boy and asked how it all happened. He told the merchant the entire story and showed him his wish granting jewel. The merchant said, "You have everything, you must be satisfied. Please give me the jewel and take all of these animals with their packs full of merchandise as well." The Brahman boy gave his wish granting jewel to the rich merchant. Then the Brahman boy slept on his soft silk mattress. The next morning, as the Brahman boy woke up, he found his bed very hard and cold. There was neither the house nor any expensive things. He was all alone in that empty strip of land. Suddenly, he became sad. Once again, his three friends came and asked, "What went wrong?" He explained how he had given the wish granting jewel to the merchant. They said, "How dare you give away such a precious jewel.? You are indeed a fool! Let us see if we can get it back." Then the three went out.

The animals saw that the merchant had become even richer. The bear and the monkey could not enter the merchant's home, so they sent the mouse to look for the jewel. The mouse entered the compound through a hole in the wood. The merchant was sleeping in a nice floored room and there was a big mound of rice. There was an arrow stuck into the center of the mound of rice. The jewel was tied to the tip of the arrow, and a cat was guarding the rice. The mouse could not go closer to the jewel. He returned to his friends and told them everything. The bear said, "We are helpless, let us go back," but the monkey interrupted, "No, I have an idea. Mouse, you go back tonight and cut off some locks of hair from the merchant's head. Tomorrow evening, he will surely move the cat and tie it to a leg of his bed. Then you can steal the jewel." The mouse did this, he nibbled on the merchant's hair locks. When the merchant woke up the next morning and moved his head, some of his hair fell down and he felt his head had become lighter. He thought it to be an inauspicious sign and said, "Alas! Last night, a mouse ate off some of my hair. Arrange

for a big prayer to guard the rest of my hair. Tie the cat to my pillow."

Again, the bear and the monkey waited near the hole and sent in the mouse to steal the gem. The mouse went in and saw that the cat was not near the mound of rice anymore. He felt very happy and tried to reach for the jewel, but could not reach up to the tip of the arrow, so he came out empty handed. The bear said, "We are helpless, let us go back." Again, the monkey interrupted and said, "You go and dig at the bottom of the mound of rice, then the arrow will fall down. Then roll the jewel to the hole that is here." The mouse did this. He rolled the jewel into the compound, but as he reached near the hole, he could not push it over a log. The mouse returned very tired to the bear and the monkey. He told them, "The jewel is near the hole, but there is this log and I can't push it anymore." The bear said, "Monkey and I can't enter the compound. We are helpless, let us go back." Then the monkey said, "There indeed is a way. Let us tie a thread to your tail. Then you hold tightly to the jewel with all of your four limbs and we'll pull the thread from the other end." They did what the monkey had planned and pulled both the mouse and the gem out together. The mouse was very tired now.

The monkey held the jewel in his mouth and he got on top of the bear, while the mouse slept in the monkey's ear. They then hurried back. On the way, there was a river. While they were crossing the knee deep river, the bear thought, "I am carrying the mouse, the monkey and the gem. I am very strong." The bear asked them, "Am I not strong?" The mouse was asleep and the monkey could not reply to the bear because he had the gem in his mouth. The bear was angry and said, "If you both don't reply. I'll throw you both into this river." The monkey was frightened and shouted, "Please, don't throw us." As he opened his mouth, he dropped the jewel into the river.

When they reached the riverbank, the monkey said to the bear, "You are a useless animal" and they began to quarrel. The mouse woke up and asked, "What's wrong?" They told him what had happened. The mouse said, "Let me try to fix things, there is

a chance. Both of you should go away from here." The mouse scurried back and forth along the riverbank and called out, "Squeak, squeak, squeak..." All the animals in the area came and asked, "What is wrong, why are you in such a hurry?" He said, "A war is imminent. It will spare neither those on the land nor the ones in the water." They asked, "What could be done?" He said, "We should build a fort here on the edge where the land and the water meet. Otherwise, there is no way." All the animals agreed and said, "We will build a fort here." The animals in the water brought out stones, while the mouse oversaw the construction of the stone fort. When the wall was about the height of a man's hand, a huge frog rolled up the jewel saying, "This is the heaviest stone." Then the mouse called the monkey and bear and told them, "Here is the wish granting jewel." The monkey was overjoyed and said, "You are such a wise mouse!" The monkey again held the jewel in his mouth, put the mouse in his ear, and he got back on the bear.

Then they arrived at the place of the Brahman boy, they found that he was almost dead due to starvation. The monkey handed him the gem. The Brahman boy said, "My three friends are very kind to me." He crossed the river and made the same wish as before. A mansion greater than a palace and with many servants spontaneously appeared there. There were different kinds of fruit trees, birds singing melodious songs and flowers blossoming all through the year. It appeared like the place never had a season of winter. It had all the wealth and riches one could ever wish for. Then the Brahman boy held the jewel in his hands and wished, "If you are truly a wish granting gem, then as I have no wife, please grant me a celestial maiden from heaven to live in my Brahma home and be my wife." Instantly, an exceptionally beautiful maiden followed by a huge group of maidservants and attendants appeared. He lived happily with his wife, and they had many handsome sons.

Prince Gautamiputra then remarked, "That man was very fortunate." As soon as the corpse heard this, he shouted, "Good,

good." The Siddhivad corpse flew away, just when they were so close and almost at the hermit cave of Acharya Nāgārjuna.

Acharya Nāgārjuna said to the prince, "Your courage is faultless. The Siddhivad corpse escaped, because this world called Jambudvīpa, does not have that much fortune. Anyway, in this life, you will become more powerful and wealthier than any other king."

Here ends the twenty-fourth Siddhivad corpse story, The Brahman's Son.

1. The caste of priest, and considered the highest of the four major castes in ancient Indic society.

25 The Trader Who Became a King

Once again, Prince Gautamiputra walked the same route and arrived at Śītavana cemetery. He caught the Siddhivad corpse, carried the corpse on his back and began his journey home. The corpse said, "The day is long and we are tired. Tell me an interesting story and I will listen. If you want me to tell you a story, just give a nod." The prince did not say a word

The Siddhivad corpse then narrated the following story:

Once upon a time, there was a king who ruled over a great kingdom. Over on the neighboring kingdom was another great king as well. A trader named Bhramaraiṣatātura[1] from the neighboring kingdom frequently did business with the kingdom on this side, so he settled down on this side of kingdom.

One day, when the trader was walking around the kingdom where he lived, he saw a man frying snacks in butter for the New Year. The trader looked through the door and saw the man eat one piece, while he dipped another piece in butter. The trader opened the door and said, "Can you please give me one of those snacks." The man said, "When all of these are fried, and they cool down, I'll give you one." The trader asked, "What did you do with the ones that you fried earlier? Give me one of those." The man thought that what he said was true and wondered if the trader was clairvoyant. The man reported this to his king, he said, "The man from the other kingdom was clairvoyant." This news spread to the other kingdom too and everyone thought the man was clairvoyant.

One day, the king from the kingdom where the man lived, lost his divine horse. The king ordered, "Bring the clairvoyant trader here." The king said, "My divine horse is lost. You should find it through the power of your clairvoyance." The trader returned to his home and he sat on the top floor of his house and invoked his Lama. Not finding any clues or a solution, he climbed up to his roof and sadly sat there.

The three men, who had stolen the king's divine horse, were actually nearby. The thieves wondered what the clairvoyant trader would say about them. As they tried to listen through a hole in the wall of the trader's house, the trader who was on the roof, saw them hiding. The trader was curious who the three persons were and what they were talking about. Sneaking quietly to the edge of the roof, he listened as the three thieves said, "They say that the trader definitely has the skill of clairvoyance. He must be aware of our presence here and might take us to the royal court tomorrow. Then what can we do?" One man said, "I doubt if he can reveal us to the king. His fame of having clairvoyance may be bogus. It is hard to say." As the trader overheard their conversation, he plucked strands of hair from a gazelle skin that was under his feet. Then he quietly sprinkled the small hairs on the heads of the men.

The next day, the trader appeared at the king's court and said, "Oh king! Let all people of this kingdom assemble. I, through the power of my clairvoyance, will reveal to you the thieves who stole your divine horse." Then the king notified the leaders of the household from sections in the tens, the hundreds, and the thousands to have all the subjects immediately assemble. Then the trader inspected each person by examining their hair. He finally found three people with gazelle hairs on their head. The trader said, "These three people stole your divine horse." They went away to get the divine horse and they returned the horse to the king. The trader then appealed, "Oh king, please do not pass death sentences on them." The king thought that the trader was truly clairvoyant. He further thought, "I should keep the trader on my side among my subjects and must not let him travel to the kingdom on the other side." The king invited the trader to his palace and offered an extended grand feast. He rewarded him richly for finding his divine horse. Moreover, the king also gave one of the princesses to the trader as his wife.

One day, a subject of the kingdom of the side where the trader lived, appeared before the king said, "I lost my three donkeys. I think they were stolen." The king summoned the clairvoyant trader and said to him, "Find the stolen donkeys using your clairvoyance." The trader thought, "In the first case, I knew about the confectioner's habit of eating by looking through his door as he prepared the snacks. The second time, I was sad and climbed up to my roof, I overheard the thieves talking about the divine horse. However, this time, if I do not run away from this kingdom, the king might punish me." As he fled towards the valley going eastwards, he saw a man running alone in the valley. Thinking this man might make a good company, he ran after the man until he caught up with him. The man, thinking that the trader was clairvoyant, turned back and bowed down nine times. Then facing the trader, he confessed, "I had nothing to eat. Therefore, I stole the donkeys. Please save me from the death sentence." The trader immediately learned that this was the man who stole the donkeys. The trader asked him, "Where are the donkeys now?" The man said, "Up there, in the hills" and he brought them down. The trader returned the donkeys and appealed to the king, "Please, forgive him and do not charge him with the death sentence." Thus, he saved the thief.

Then one day, the king lost his life turquoise[2] gem and he again summoned the trader to the palace. The king said, "I lost my life turquoise gem. You should find it through the power of your clairvoyance." The trader thought, "In the first case, I knew about the confectioner's habit by looking through the door as he prepared the snacks. The second time, as I was sad and climbed to the roof, I overheard the thieves talking about the divine horse. The third time, I just ran towards the valley and learned about the thief who stole the donkeys. However, this time, if I do not run away from this kingdom, the king might punish me." So he returned home.

It so happened that one of the King's most trusted ministers named Harśa[3] stole the king's life turquoise gem. Fearing execution if the trader revealed to the king about the life turquoise gem, he was unsure of what to do. Around midnight, he got up and aimlessly walked behind the trader's house. He listened through a hole in the trader's house. He was worried about what he should tell the king this time. Because he lacked any true clairvoyance, he was helpless. Deeply saddened and missing his old father, whose name was Harśa, he cried, "Oh Harśa!" This is how he kept crying while facing the wall in his house. The minister, Harśa heard this from behind the wall and he immediately entered the trader's house. He cried, "Your honor, I am here." The trader felt happy and said, "Harśa! Please come inside." As the minister came in, he revealed to the trader, "I committed this crime, just like a man who had lost his way in broad daylight. Overcome by ignorance, I stole the king's life turquoise gem. Please save the kingdom and my life too." The trader then said, "Bring the life turquoise gem here." The minister gave it to the trader, who then walked to the palace. He offered the life turquoise gem back to the king and said, "Through the power of my clairvoyance, I knew that your minister, Harśa had stolen it out of sheer ignorance. He has been very kind to me. So, please do not punish him." The king was very pleased to get his life turquoise gem back. The king rewarded the trader greatly and as requested, the king did not punish the minister.

One day, the trader said to his wife, "Please bring a jar of rice wine." He went to sleep in a dark corner in his room. After that, his wife served the wine to him. Revealing his true self, he said, "In the first case, I knew about the confectioner's habit by looking through the door as he prepared the snacks. The second time, as I was sad and climbed the roof and I overheard the thieves talking about the divine horse. The third time, I just ran towards the valley and learned about the thief that stole the donkeys. Then crying for my old father Harśa, who I greatly missed, I recovered your father's life turquoise gem. So far, as a trader I just roamed around. Now it is better that I return to my other kingdom." The princess became angry. She ran to the king and cried out, "Oh

Lord! My husband doesn't seem to be of a good parentage." Then she told the entire story she had heard from her husband. However, the king said, "Your husband, the trader, is a wise man with unequaled clairvoyance. Only a man of so good a parentage would be suitable as your spouse." The princess again refused to accept him as her husband. At that time, a wise minister said, "In the past, the trader possessed all these characters and was with you for a long time. How come you did not have any complaints back then? Anyway, let me examine your husband thoroughly."

Minister Harśa took his midday meal and walked across the mountain pass. He looked in all four directions and saw not a single person anywhere. Wild animals moved here and there and birds flew around. He saw a bee buzzing over a flower. The minister caught it, wrapped it in five colors of silk cloth and brought it with him.

Every person in the kingdom was asked to come to the palace and they all assembled before the king. The king sat on the golden throne. The trader was also notified to come. The princess was present too. When the trader arrived, the minister said, "Oh trader with unrestricted clairvoyance. I walked across the pass, unseen even by wild animals or birds. I found this, which is in my hand. You should know what this is." The trader said to them, "First, I knew about the confectioner's habit by looking through the door as he prepared the snacks. The second time, as I was sad, I climbed the roof and overheard the thieves talking about the divine horse. The third time, I just ran towards the valley and learned about the thief who stole the donkeys. Then crying for my old father Harśa, who I miss, I recovered the king's life turquoise gem. But today, I am sure that I know it is a live bee buzzing in the minister's hand." The minister laughed, "Ha! Ha!" Then he said, "Everyone and the princess too. Come and see what I have here. Behind the pass, unseen by even the birds and wild animals, I caught a bee buzzing and encircling a bunch of flowers. Now let us check if the bee is alive, as the trader claims." Then he unfolded the silk clothes, one by one. The bee flew away into the air. The king, the ministers and the king's subjects were all convinced that the trader did have the power of clairvoyance.

Then, the trader and the princess ruled the kingdom, fully committing their lives to their royal duties. Their subjects were happier and wealthier than before.

Prince Gautamiputra remarked, "How lucky was the trader! Everything went so well for him." Immediately the corpse said, "The unfortunate prince spoke." The Siddhivad corpse slapped the prince three times and flew away, like before.

Here ends the twenty-fifth Siddhivad corpse story, The Trader Who Became a King.

---

1. Tib. Sprang ma gzir chung (Skt. Bhramaraiṣatātura) means indistinct sound.
2. See Story 11.
3. Tib. ḥa śa.

26 The Sword of Vajrapāṇi

Once again, Prince Gautamiputra walked the same route and arrived at Śītavana cemetery. He caught the Siddhivad corpse and carried the corpse on his back and began his journey back home. The corpse said, "The day is long and we are tired. Tell me an interesting story and I will listen. If you want me to tell you a story, just give a nod." The prince did not say a word.

The Siddhivad corpse then narrated the following story:

Once, there lived a king, who ruled a kingdom in the upper part of the region. The king had two princes. The elder prince was unintelligent, while the younger prince was very smart and intelligent. After their parents died, the younger prince ruled the kingdom from the palace, while the elder prince was given a separate house to live in.

The elder prince earned his livelihood from farming. Once, he was very worried, as he had no seeds to sow in his field. The elder prince recited the mantras to invoke Lord Vajrapāṇi.[1] One night, while the elder prince was asleep, he had a dream where a voice said to him, "Oh prince, a sword of a special size is very valuable." Then the next day, a rich man from the neighborhood came to him with a jar of wine and a sword. The rich man bowed down to the elder prince, served the wine and said, "This sword is the most valuable thing I have, it was my father's sword. As you are unable to sow the field, I don't know, but would like to exchange your field for my family sword? It would be beneficial for both of us to do this. This has been prophesied to me." The elder prince asked, "What were you foretold?" The rich man answered, "In my sleep, I dreamed that if I gave this sword to the elder prince from the upper valley, he will assume great powers." The elder prince realized then that what he saw in his dream was the same prophecy given to this rich man too. He took the sword and he leased his field to the man for a few years. The rich man was very happy and returned to the lower valley. The elder prince was satisfied for having received the sword. One night, through the blessings of Lord Vajrapāṇi and the merits accumulated through chanting mantras, the elder prince received another prophecy. It said, "Take this sword and go to the land beyond the high mountain pass. There you have a great purpose to accomplish!"

The elder prince climbed the high mountain pass and gazed down the slope. He saw many red faced people. Thinking it must be a big feast, he walked towards the gathering. As he went further, he saw people throwing dice. The elder prince watched them and saw three men playing with the dice had lost the game. Then their relatives surrounded them and began to cry. The villagers gave them different kinds of food, but the three men looked very sad. The elder prince asked, "What is wrong? Why are these three men looking so sad?" The villagers said, "They have done no wrong. Once there was a great king and a queen in this kingdom. They had a princess, attendants and subjects. When the king and queen died, their spirits remained attached to the princess. The evil spirits that possesed the princess has already devoured all the ministers and the attendants in the palace. Now we have to give up three people everyday to the evil spirits. We decide who is to go by throwing dice." The elder prince thought, "These relatives of the three condemned men looked very sad, I have nobody who will cry for me. How good I could be if I take their place. I'll be able to help and free them from their grief and sorrow." He said to the three men, "Don't be sad. I'll go instead of you." The three men and their relatives were very pleased. They bowed down to him repeatedly as they did to the Maṇḍala of Buddha Bhaiṣajya.[2] The villagers served him the best food. The elder prince then headed towards the palace.

As the elder prince reached the palace gate, he could hear no sounds of either humans or dogs. He climbed the wide stairs and reached the main hall. There he saw more than one hundred beheaded bodies on the right side and about one hundred mutilated bodies on the left side. The elder prince saw that the demons had killed many people, but still he could not see the evil spirits. As he recited the Vajrapāṇi mantra and climbed another set of stairs, he found himself in front of a huge door. He opened that door and walked in. He found himself in a hall of eight columns and in the center of them was a turquoise throne. On the throne sat a very beautiful girl, about eighteen years of age, resting under a warm sheep skin blanket. The elder prince looked in all directions, but he could see nothing else, except a locked door. He still wondered where the killer demons could be. He went up to the roof, but they were not there also.

The elder prince went back to the hall and walked towards the princess, who was sleeping on the turquoise throne and he stood by the pillow. He tugged at the pillow, but got no response from the girl. He checked and found that she was still breathing, but was in a very miserable condition. Then he cut off a piece of meat, put some butter on it and made a cake as big as a head. Then sitting close to the throne, he began to eat. It was already lunch time now. The girl in the room lifted her head and turned towards to look around. He turned to look and his sword almost came out from its sheath by itself. He wondered why the girl was in such weak health and he wondered where the spirits of the dead could be. Then he sat down reciting the Vajrapāṇi mantra.

As the sun set behind the mountains, the girl turned in her throne. Again, the sword moved and shook lightly inside the sheath. Then she suddenly sprang up with fear. From among the beams, he heard two sounds, "Ding, dong." Then from the girl's nose two vicious snakes emerged. As the elder prince saw the snakes, he was frightened and stood up. The sword said to the prince, "Prince, sit down." As the snakes came out from her nose, the elder prince drew out the sword from the sheath and killed the snakes. Thus, he killed the spirits of the deceased royal couple. The elder prince asked the girl, "Where have those two snakes gone?" The girl replied, "The snakes heads were cut off and they are here near the handle of your sword." The elder prince again removed his sword and found pieces of a snake body clinging on the blade. The sword said to the prince, "I have killed the spirits of the dead." The sword that spoke in a human voice was in fact a manifestation of Vajrapāṇi. The girl asked the elder prince, "Are you a man with a kingdom or one without a kingdom? You do not seem to be from my kingdom." The elder prince just looked at her and could say nothing. Then the sword said, "He has a kingdom and he is a good man. He is the prince born of a king of high nobility. It is his good fortune that he came to this kingdom, I am here to help both of you." The girl said, "Did you inherit this sword from your ancestors? Where did you get this nice sword?" He replied, "Don't speak about the extraordinary powers of this sword to anyone. When you move around, keep the sword close to you. While sleeping, tuck it under your pillow. It will guard you at all times. It shall support you forever."

Then, the next day, the villagers gathered, and someone said, "The man who went to the palace instead of our three men must have been eaten by the evil spirits. We must now cast the dice again and decide who should go next." As they were casting the dice and praying, the elder prince arrived and said, "Now you don't need the dice anymore. Just come to the palace and check it out." The villagers thought, "He is a stranger, yesterday he helped us, but today he might be deceiving us." They suspected that the demons sent him to lure all the people into the palace and they hesitated to go. However, a wise man among them said, "We should send someone to go and see." They asked one man, "You go to the palace first and we will follow you later." So, they sent one man in advance to the palace before they all went.

The man that the villagers sent came into the room in the palace where the elder prince was. There was nobody there except the elder prince and the princess. He bowed down to them as one does before the Maṇḍala of Buddha Bhaiṣajya. Then he returned and described everything he saw to the villagers. All the subjects of that kingdom rejoiced and entered the palace to pay their respects to the elder prince and their princess.

The elder prince married the princess and ruled over the kingdom. From among the people, who came to the palace to pay their respect, the elder prince appointed the elderly ones as his senior ministers. The king ruled the kingdom according to the principles of the Dharma. The kingdom thrived with greater prosperity and happiness. He gave his own house and his field of land to the rich man, who he earlier leased the field to in exchange for the sword. The two kingdoms functioned as one kingdom, but enjoyed their own sovereign autonomy.

Then Prince Gautamiputra said, "It was the Vajrapāṇi mantra that actually helped the king." The corpse said, "The unfortunate prince finally spoke." The Siddhivad corpse slapped the prince three times and the Siddhivad corpse disappeared.

Here ends the twenty-sixth Siddhivad corpse story, The Sword of Vajrapāṇi.

1. Tib. Phyag rdor (Skt. Vajrapāṇi) literally Vajra-holder, a Bodhisattva who is invoked primarily for subduing our afflictive emotion of desire and attachment.
2. Tib. Sman bla (Skt. Bhaiṣajya Buddha) is widely acclaimed as the Medicine Buddha and is prayed for the alleviation of all suffering and pain associated with sickness and disease.

27 The Wise Minister

Once again, Prince Gautamiputra returned to the Śītavana cemetery to catch the Siddhivad corpse. The prince walked to the tree and shouted, "Will you come down or do I cut down this tree?" He took out his sword and waved it in the sky. The corpse hesitantly climbed down. The prince hit the corpse all over, from head to toe. He tied the neck and the legs of the corpse together with a rope and forced him into the bag. Then the prince began his journey back to the hermit's area. After having barely taken ten steps, the corpse said, "Prince, Prince." The prince knew what he was after and did not reply. The corpse said, "It is a surprise that I met a prince like you. You speak not a single word from your mouth. I will tell you a very interesting story, maybe more interesting than the earlier ones. So listen."

The Siddhivad corpse then narrated the following story:

Once, there lived a king, who ruled over a kingdom in eastern India. The king had two princes. One was clever and intelligent, while the other was not. After the king and the queen died, the younger prince being the clever and intelligent one, was enthroned as the king. The elder prince was unintelligent and the people of the kingdom disliked him. There was, however, a wise minister, who knew that the elder prince was not a good speaker and was hated by everyone in the kingdom. However, the minister also knew that the elder prince was destined to be very fortunate in the near future, so he remained the elder prince's personal attendant.

One day, the wise minister said to the elder prince, "Your highness, today you should go and enjoy the scenery around the big lake at the end of the valley." The elder prince agreed and went to the lake shore. Around midday, waves in the lake began to rise higher and higher. The prince was amazed at this strange behavior and kept watching. Then a beautiful maiden of the lake, wearing an aquamarine silk appeared. Holding a tray made of conch shells in her right hand and a golden ladle in her left, she came up riding an elephant. She sprinkled white sparkling water. The elder prince found her very pretty. Then she disappeared back into the water and the prince returned home. The minister came to him and asked, "What scenery did you see today?" The elder prince explained, "There was a wonderful sight to see. In our lake, I saw a beautiful maiden of the lake. As I looked from her right side, she seemed to be bending backwards. When I looked from her left side, she seemed to be leaning forward. She was like a flower bending back and forth. Sunshine seemed to melt around her, while a cold breeze seemed to freeze her. She was like a rainbow, wearing five shades of aquamarine silk. Holding a tray made of conch shells in her left hand and a golden ladle in her right, she was also riding on an elephant. How nice it would be if I could get her as my life partner." The minister said, "If you could gather information about her birth place and her parents, it will be easy."

Then after a few days, the minister said to the prince, "Today is an auspicious day for you, as I see a friendly combination between the stars and the planets. So, go to the lake now. You might be able to see that girl again. If you see her, you should ask about her birthplace, her parent's name and her name too. Go now." Then the elder prince arrived at the lake at around the same time of the day as before. The waves moved and he watched and waited eagerly. Like the last time, the girl appeared again. When he asked her, "Where do you come from?" She pointed her finger to the elephant. When he asked, "What is your father's name?" She pointed to her nose. Then the prince asked, "What is your mother's name?" She pointed to her footwear. Then he asked, "Who are you?" In response, she pointed her finger to her head. She drank milk and disappeared back into the lake.

The elder prince then returned home. The minister asked him, "What did that girl tell you?" He said, "She didn't say a word." The minister asked, "Did she make any gestures?" He said, "Yes,

she made a few gestures. When I asked where she is from, she pointed at the elephant. When I asked for her father's name, she pointed to her nose. When I asked for her mother's name, she pointed at her footwear. When I asked who she was, she pointed to her head." The wise minister understood the meanings and said, "We can solve this." The minister deciphered what all the gestures meant and told them, "When she pointed her finger to the elephant, she meant that she is from the kingdom of Hastisānu.[1] When she pointed her finger to her nose, she meant she is the princess of King Guṇapara.[2] When she pointed her finger to her footwear, she meant that her mother is Māyadevī.[3] And, when she pointed her finger to her head, she introduced herself as Princess Śiravata.[4] See, the puzzle is solved." The minister and the prince were both happy.

Then, after a few days, the elder prince and the minister loaded their belongings on an elephant. The prince rode on the elephant and headed towards the Indian kingdom of Hastisānu. There were many ferocious beasts on their way. However, due to having accumulated many merits in his previous lives, they were fortunate to have the beasts welcome them. Then they finally saw the kingdom of Hastisānu from afar. There was a rocky mountain, as sharp as a sword with a cave nearby. The minister remained in the cave and said to the prince, "Today you go alone from here, the girl will come to the eastern gate of the palace. You should go there and ask if anyone wishes to play chess."[5] She will oblige you and she will come to play. So, while you play the game, you have to say, "Obeisance to Guru Padmasambhava[6] of Uddyan.[7] May the five ḍākinīs[8] be subdued." Then the minister placed one pebble on the ground in the center of the cave. Also, the minister said, "Then she might ask, 'Did you come from the Uddyana in the west?' You must only say, 'I have never been to the land of Uddyana. But I am Dorje Droloe'.[9] Then say nothing more. When the girl places a mattress, sit squarely and say, 'Triple gem, I first offer my seat to you!' If she serves you wine, you must say, 'Triple gem, I first offer my wine to you.' Then if she asks you, 'Where do the Mahasiddhas[10] of the eight cemeteries dwell?' Just say, 'I am

Dorje Droloe, the master of the eight cemeteries.' Gaze at her with your eyes wide open."

The elder prince went to the east gate of the palace and did what the minister had taught him. For a while, the princess jumped around here and there. The elder prince said, "Oh girl, calm down and don't be so impatient." Then the princess bowed down to the prince and said, "Oh emanated one, please save me." The princess served him well. After three to four days, she doubted if he could be the same prince that she saw on the lake shore of Mahāsuka.[11]

After 15 days, the minister, who lived in the cave, had run out of all his provisions. Disguising himself as a diviner, he carried few clothes over his shoulder and walked towards the palace of Hastisānu. People of Hastisānu consulted the diviner. The maids of the princess asked him, "Here is a diviner. Would you like to consult with our princess?" The princess arranged a dre[12] of white barley, tea, molasses and other kinds of food such as rib marrow and roasted flour. When she was about to go to the diviner. The elder prince asked, "Oh princess, where are you going?" The princess said, "I am going to consult a diviner." The elder prince suddenly remembered the minister and said, "Let me come with you to the diviner as well." The princess said, "Then why don't we invite him in to see us?" A maid went to the diviner and told him, "Please come inside the palace. Our queen and her friend want to consult with you?"

As requested, the minister, disguised as a diviner, arrived on the upper storey of the palace. The elder prince recognized the minister and suddenly got up. But the diviner winked at him and hinted to do nothing. The elder prince sat down in a serious posture. Then the diviner paid his respects to him. The elder prince responded saying, "Welcome, diviner." The princess then gave him the articles for divination and asked, "Please conduct a divination for our entire family." The diviner said, "The princess's mind is nervous. I see that he is the prince of Mahāsuka and a real emanation of Guru Padmasambhava. In this kingdom of Hastisānu, the great king Guṇapara rules magnificently. Do they have a lot of good wealth and prosperity? The snow lion will come on the snowy mountains and turquoise gems will spread in the four directions. The turquoise dragon will float in the sky and the sound of fame will spread to all of the four continents."

The diviner then stood up to leave. However, the princess was highly pleased and she offered to pay a fee and give gifts. She asked the diviner to stay in the palace. The diviner said to the elder prince, "You might stay here for another few days. If the princess serves you wine, you should refuse to drink unless she brings wine for herself too. The princess will bring two identical small drinking glasses. Then put this pill for forgetfulness into the glass near her pillow and keep it near her. Until you go to bed that night, leave the wine near your pillow. Tell the princess that you drank from her glass. To the ministers and the maids, who get close to the princess, tell them that the princess is seriously ill and that they should not go near her anymore. Order only two maids to attend to her. Then ask her to call the diviner and leave the rest to me." Then the minister returned to the cave.

The elder prince did as the diviner had taught him. The princess brought two identical tumblers of wine. She kept one for the prince and the other near her bed. When the princess was away lighting the lamps, the elder prince secretly put the pill into her glass. About midnight, the elder prince told others about the princess falling unconscious and he called for the diviner. As the diviner arrived, he opened all the treasures and loaded up many elephants with gold, silver, precious gems, silk and fabric woven with elaborate designs. He loaded one elephant with a wooden seat frame and sat the princess in it. He then poured wine and drugged all the caretakers in the elephant barn and in the horse barn and the maids too. They all got drunk and slept. He took the chief maid on the elephant to attend to the princess. With elephants loaded with gold, silver and precious gems etc, they left for the city of Mahāsuka.

When they were almost a day away from their palace in Mahāsuka, the princess woke up and felt as if awakened from a deep slumber. She found herself in an unknown land with the

prince and the diviner. The princess knew that it was not her kingdom, but she was helpless. So, she said, "You have been very lucky, but you can't rule two kingdoms. My parents have no sons. Therefore, you should not rule this kingdom, but better to return to rule my father's kingdom."

At around that time, all the attendants in the palace of Hastisānu recovered from their being intoxicated. They found that the treasury doors were open. So, they locked and sealed all the doors. As they could not find the prince and the princess, they said, "That diviner has told us that this kingdom would prosper, but being in such a state now, how can it be prosperous?" Then all the attendants went to report these events to king Guṇapara. The king and the queen became very worried. They asked four ministers to undertake a search mission. The ministers arrived at the palace of Mahāsuka and they talked to the wise minister. They negotiated with each other about how they would rule the kingdoms. The prince and the princess decided to rule the kingdom of Hastisānu, while the younger prince and his ministers ruled the kingdom of Mahāsuka. The king and the queen were active doing spiritual practices, while the two princes led their respective kingdoms to great prosperity.

Prince Gautamiputra said, "For the elder prince, who knew nothing, the minister has been very kind and helpful." Immediately, the corpse shouted, "The unfortunate prince finally spoke." He slapped the prince three times and the Siddhivad corpse fled away.

Here ends the twenty-seventh Siddhivad corpse story, The Wise Minister.

1. Tib. Glang po gshong pa (Skt. Hastisānu), means elephant valley.
2. Tib. Gurna pa ra (Skt. Guṇapara), means one with noble qualities.

3. Tib. Sgyu ma lha mdzes (Skt. Māyadevī), means divine enchantress.
4. Tib. Dbu ldan (Skt. Śiravata), means one with a head.
5. Tib. Phren, a checker board game similar to chess.
6. Tib. Orgyen padma 'byung gnas (Skt. Padmasambhava), an Indian tantric master who visited Tibet for the propagation of Buddhism during the reign of Tibetan emperor Trisong Detsen (742-797).
7. Tib. Orgyen (Skt. Uddyana), considered the birthplace of Tantric master Padmasambhava, but scholars disagree on its actual location.
8. Tib. Mkha' 'gro (Skt. dākinī), literally meaning sky-goer, is a class of celestial being.
9. Tib. Rdo rje gro lod, one of the many emanations of the Guru Padmasambhava and counted as one of his eight main emanations.
10. Tib. Grub chen (Skt. Mahasiddha), means a great accomplished ascetic.
11. Tib. Bde ldan (Skt. Mahāsuka), means joyous one.
12. Tib. Bre ga, a unit of volume used in Tibet and measuring approximately 250 grams.

28 Lady Kaphalikālaghu

Once again, Prince Gautamiputra returned to Śītavana cemetery to catch the Siddhivad corpse. The prince walked up to the tree and shouted, "Will you come down or do I cut down this tree?" He took out his sword and waved it in the sky. The corpse hesitantly climbed down. The prince hit the corpse all over, from head to toe. He tied the neck and the legs of the corpse together with a rope and forced the corpse into the bag. Then the prince began his journey back to the hermit's area. After having barely taken ten steps, the corpse said, "Prince, Prince." The prince knew what he was after and did not reply. The corpse said, "It is a surprise that I met a prince like you. You speak not a single word through your mouth. I will tell you a very interesting story, maybe more interesting than the earlier ones. So listen."

The Siddhivad corpse then narrated the following story:

Once upon a time, there lived an old man, an old woman and their three daughters. The old couple looked after a herd of yaks and a flock of sheep.

One day, the old man herded his sheep to the back of a mountain pass. A demon killed the old man and ate him. The demon also killed and ate a black sheep. The demon skinned the old man's head and wore it over his own head. Then he drove the flock of sheep back to the old man's home. When the old woman came to receive the sheep, the demon, who was disguised as the old man, said to her, "My wife, I have decided that tomorrow, I will give our eldest daughter to a rich man across the pass. Today I killed a black sheep for the wedding food and I drank wine. This is your share." He then gave her a fat kidney from the old man. The old woman roasted the kidney and was about to eat it, when the demon said, "The old woman, who eats her husband's flesh." The old woman asked, "Oh my husband, what do you mean by that?" The demon said, "I mean, the kidney is getting burned." The old woman did not know that the kidney belonged to her husband and she ate it.

The next day, the demon took the eldest daughter to tend to the sheep behind the mountain pass. He killed her and ate her and then placed her head near her father's head. The demon then killed a white sheep and ate it. In the evening the demon came home with the sheep and with a kidney from the eldest daughter. As the old woman came to receive the sheep, the demon said, "I have agreed that tomorrow I will give our second daughter to a rich man across the pass. I killed a white sheep for the wedding food and I drank wine. This is your share." So the demon handed over a kidney from the eldest daughter. The old woman roasted the kidney and was about to eat it, when the demon said, "You are an old woman who eats her child's flesh." The old woman asked, "Oh my husband, what do you mean by this?" The demon said, "I mean that the kidney is getting burned." The old woman did not know that was the kidney of her eldest daughter and she ate it.

The next day, the demon took the second daughter to tend the sheep behind the pass. He killed and ate her and then placed her head near her father's head. The demon then killed a white sheep and ate it. In the evening the demon came home with a kidney from the second daughter and the sheep. As the old woman came to receive the sheep, the demon said, "My wife, I have decided that tomorrow I will give our youngest daughter to a rich man across the pass. I killed one sheep for the wedding food and I drank wine. This is your share." Then, like before, he handed her a fat kidney from the second daughter. The old woman said, "We can't give away our youngest daughter. We need her to serve us when we are older." Then the old man said, "If we are healthy, we can have another daughter anytime. Let us give her away." The last daughter, being the youngest, was very dear and close to the old woman. So the old woman became very sad. She made a lot of butter food and gave it to her youngest daughter. Then she said, "What a pity!" The old woman wondered what her old man was really doing.

The next day, the old woman was overcome by sorrow, she found it hard to let her daughter go. However, the old man took her away by force. The youngest daughter, in her previous life, was a girl that had devoted her life to reciting the Hayagrīva[1] mantra. But at one point, she lost faith about the power and quality of Hayagrīva. After that she took rebirth as the poor old couple's daughter. The demon and youngest daughter arrived at the place where the head of the old man was on the ground. The demon said, "Sit here, while I will see if the man you are to marry has come." Then, the demon went away.

After a while, a spotted puppy came to the youngest daughter and said, "Girl, if you give me some of your food, I will tell you a story. If you give me more food, I will tell you two stories. If you give me all of your food, I will tell you all the stories." Deeply stricken by her sorrow, she had no appetite for food and she gave all of her food to the puppy. Then the puppy said, "He is not your real father, he is a demon. The head of your father and of your two sisters are lying over there." The puppy showed them to the youngest daughter. As she saw the heads, she was very frightened and asked the puppy, "Is there any way I can escape from the demon?" The puppy said, "I pity you, I'll tell you how to remove the evil demon." The puppy handed her an iron pan and said, "Take this pan and quietly escape down the pass. The demon will tell you to stop running and that he is your real father. When he comes to catch you, roll this iron pan down from the mountain pass and follow wherever it goes. Run and never look back. Then you will be saved." Then the puppy disappeared. The puppy was in fact a manifestation of Hayagrīva, who she worshipped in her previous live.

The youngest daughter took the iron pan and escaped down the pass. The demon chased her and cried out, "My daughter! Your father is here. Where are you going?" She ran further and as the demon chased her, she threw the iron pan. She shouted, "Oh pan! roll down!" Then she kept running. The iron pan rolled into a big heap of yak dung and she followed it. There she saw a closed wooden door. She opened it and there was another closed door made of iron. She opened that and again she saw a door with many jewels. As she entered that door, there was a room with stairs, she went up to an upper floor. There was nobody there, only a rooster sitting near another door. The rooster said, "Cluck! Cluck! Welcome girl. You must be very tired. Enter the storeroom and eat meat, butter, cheese, cake or whatever pleases you." She walked into the storeroom and ate meat and butter until she was full.

After a few days, the rooster said, "Inside the treasury room, there is clothing and jewelry. Put them on and go to the lower valley to enjoy a feast at a fair." The youngest daughter took the clothing and the jewelry, put them on and looked very nice. After the girl went away, the rooster saddled a nice horse that he had kept hidden in the courtyard. At this point, the rooster took off his bird covering, rolled it up and put it between the beams in the room. Having put on a nice set of clothes and jewelry too, he left to go to the same fair. The rooster-man rode around on his horse at the market in a clockwise direction. He did not see anyone there who was more beautiful than the youngest daughter. The youngest daughter walked around the market in a counterclockwise direction. She did not see anyone there who was more handsome than the man riding his blue horse. To avoid the people from recognizing him, the man filled one side of the saddlebag with molasses and the other bag with dust and scattered them around as he rode. As people jumped for the molasses, they spread the dust in the air and this temporarily blocked their vision. He whipped his horse and visualized Hayagrīva on the crown of his head and he reached the top of the valley. There he took off the saddle and hid his horse in the compound. He also hid the clothing and jewelry. He put on his bird covering and sat down reciting Hayagrīva's mantra as the girl returned. The rooster said, "Welcome girl, did you spend the whole day in the market? Who was the most handsome man and who was the most beautiful lady?" She replied, "A man called Kukkutahingula[2] from the upper valley was the most handsome man and as for ladies, there

were many pretty ones." The rooster said, "You must be hungry. Now eat meat and butter." She ate the food and served the rooster too.

After a few days, the rooster asked the youngest daughter, "Dress up again and put on the jewelry and go to the market." She put on the clothing and the jewelry and left for the fair. He also dressed up and adorned himself with jewels as before and he followed her. He rode around the market and found that the youngest daughter was the prettiest of all. The youngest daughter saw no man as handsome as the one she saw the other day. People in the market said, "A man named Kukkutahingula was carried away by a local spirit, because he was a great speaker. This girl is so pretty." Then the rooster-man got up as before and threw molasses and dust around. People did not see what direction he had gone to. As he arrived back in the upper valley, he hid his horse and his clothes and jewelry like before. He sat at home reciting the Hayagrīva mantra as the girl returned. The rooster said, "Welcome girl, did you spend the whole day in the market? Who was the most handsome man and who was the most beautiful lady?" She replied, "A man called Kukkutahingula from the upper valley was the most handsome man and as for the ladies there were many pretty ones." The rooster said, "You must be hungry. Now eat meat and butter." She ate the food and served the rooster too.

One day, the rooster again said, "Girl, go to the market in the lower valley and watch the fair." The youngest daughter thought, "Kukkutahingula whom the demons carried to the upper valley must be this rooster. She wore the clothes and jewelry as before, but this time, hid herself in the courtyard. Then she saw the rooster remove his bird covering and store it between the beams. She also saw him put on his nice clothes and his jewelry. He turned into a man that was very handsome to behold. He then left for the market. After he left, the youngest daughter burned his bird covering to ashes. She thought that "If this bird covering was lost, then I could spent the rest of my life with this extremely handsome man." The man rode around the market twice, in a clockwise and a counterclockwise direction, but he did not see the youngest daughter there. As usual, the man threw molasses and dust around the area and he rode home.

As the man found what she had done, he said to her, "It's not good that you burned my bird covering. It would have been possible for you to stay as my spouse, if I wore that bird covering for only five more years. But now there is no way we can have each other." Then she sobbed and asked, "What truly was that bird covering? Is there anything we can do?" He said, "I am the prince of a king, who ruled at the back of this valley. My father died a long time ago. As the most handsome of all humans, I lived with my mother, the queen, our subjects and our wealth. It has been prophesied that I would be taken away by the local spirits and demons. However, it said that if I stayed here in this house, disguised as a bird for ten years and I recited the Hayagrīva mantra, I could be immune to the local ghosts and demons. The queen mother and others back home do not know that I am here. Now, I can't get another bird covering, I can't live here, as the local ghosts will soon come to take me away." She embraced him and wept and asked, "Is there anything, even now, that I could do?" He said, "As you are pregnant and carrying my child, walk down the valley. Go to the tall fort decorated with huge antlers on the roof. Take this Hayagrīva statue with you, which is my meditation object and recite the mantra. My dog will receive you there. On a round platform, you will see my old mother, the queen. As she welcomes you, tell her about yourself and then stay there."

The youngest daughter went down the valley and walked inside the fort as she was told. Two dogs came to receive her. The old mother saw the girl that was a stranger but the two dogs nodded their heads and wagged their tails at her. The old mother came to receive her and said, "Welcome, my girl." The youngest daughter said, "Mother, how are you?" The mother then invited her into the house and served tea. As the youngest daughter was reciting the Hayagrīva mantra, the old mother heard, "Hoolu, hoolu..." The old mother said, "Are you worried about something. Why you are you uttering that strange sound, Hoolu, hoolu? What

brought you here?" The old mother said, "Long ago, I had a young and handsome son, but I have not seen him for the last five years. I don't know where he is. He had a very similar statue that you have at your side." The girl could not control her tears and said, "I am an unfortunate girl. My two elder sisters were killed by a demon, but I was able to escape." The old mother said, "I'm sorry, if what you are saying is true" and she wept too. Then she said, "Being a woman and a mother, it is a pity that I have not seen my dear son for five years. But, you have more reasons to be sad."

The old mother let her stay in a small room and asked her to spin wool and to weave cloth. She placed the Hayagrīva statue on a high place. She took butter as her payment for weaving the cloth and spinning the wool and then made a butter lamp to offer to the statue. She continued reciting the Hayagrīva mantra. The small spotted dog that rescued her years before was in fact a manifestation of Hayagrīva. In her previous birth, she had doubted the power of Hayagrīva and that she had stopped reciting the mantra. She was thus born as a girl in a poor family. After a few months, her belly began to grow bigger and bigger. One of the maids was jealous of her and said to the old mother, "The girl in our place seems to be pregnant."

After five months, the youngest daughter finally completed her Hayagrīva meditation. One day at dawn, Hayagrīva appeared in the form of a scary looking man dressed in a tiger skin and wearing a horse's head over his head. The manifestation cried, "Hoolu...Krodha" and made other weird sounds. Then Lord Hayagrīva said, "Why did you call me?" She cried, "I can clearly recall all my previous lives." The girl then requested, "I have tried in my previous lives to invoke you through meditation. By your power, virtue and blessings from my offerings and accomplishments of meditation. May you help me bring my life partner back." Thus, she bowed down low. Hayagrīva said, "On auspicious days, make incense offerings to the deer antler. Be careful, do not mix the bowls. Visualize myself sitting above your head as before and I'll help you reunite with your husband." Then he disappeared. She continued reciting the Hayagrīva mantra as she did before.

The maid then said again to the old mother, "This girl seems to be pregnant." However, the youngest daughter said, "There is no one with me, except for the statue of this noble lord. I had many dreams last night. I have to burn incense to the deer antlers and make an elaborate purification ritual. If you help me and I also get help from the shepherds and the stable keepers, we can perform this great ritual." Others said, "What this strange girl is saying may not be true." So she returned to her small room.

Then after a few days, a red man riding a red horse with a red dog arrived at her door and said, "Oh Kaphalikālaghu,[3] my girl, listen to me. Do you have a soft pillow for your head? Do you have a cushion mattress under you and blankets over you? Have you stored barley wine near your bed and nice food to eat?" The youngest daughter said, "Kukkutahingula, I have no soft pillow for my head, but only sash and clothes for a pillow. I have a bed in a small room. I have no cushion mattress under me and no blankets over me. The clothes I wear during the day become my nightdress. I get neither any good food nor sweet barley wine to store near my bed."

Then the man came inside the room and they shared their stories. The youngest daughter asked, "Why don't you come home now?" He said, "How can I? You burned my bird covering and I was taken away by the local ghosts." She said, "How did you manage to come here today?" He said, "As soon as I was taken by the local ghost for my good looks, he made me the manager of his kitchen. Then he made me manager of his private chamber. Last time, I sent someone to bring bed wine and the wine vase slipped from his hand and the local ghost did not get his share of bed wine. He was angry and made me the stable man. In that way, I could manage to get a horse and come here. Now, we might be able to see each other again." She said, "It is good that we could meet, but do you need to go back again?" He said, "I can't say if I should go. However, make sure you tell my mother that you are carrying my child. You may get a cushioned mattress to spread underneath and a blanket to cover you." She said, "I won't until you come back again. But don't worry, as I will be fine." Then at dawn, he returned to the ghost house. The youngest daughter knew that it all happened through the blessings of Lord Hayagrīva and she prayed with more faith and a greater sincerity.

Then one early morning, Hayagrīva appeared to her and said, "My daughter, don't sleep. Get up, now." She sprang to her feet and bowed low to him. Hayagrīva said, "Today is an auspicious day. Arrange offerings and offer them to me in the morning. In the afternoon, you should hold a deer antler in your right hand and hold this small turquoise gem in your mouth. Without letting go off the antler from your hand or the turquoise gem from your mouth, visualize me on the crown of your head. You will see a hundred red soldiers on horses to the right and about a thousand on the left. At the center will be a giant man with a scorpion head standing as high as a mountain. Keep the doors closed and sit on the edge of the roof. Continue visualizing me on the crown of your head. This will fulfill the purpose you asked me the last time I was here." Then he disappeared.

Then the youngest daughter arranged the offerings. Having popped the small turquoise gem into her mouth and held the antler in her hand, she visualized Hayagrīva on her head. The mental aspect of Hayagrīva manifested in the form of a blue horse and sat near the spring. Then she saw the prince arriving, carrying a copper vase on his back with an apron placed underneath and a ladle in his hand. The prince then said, "Flee far from this red cliff. The dungeon of the local demon is gloomy. In the small square shaped fortress of the deer antlers, the lady Kaphalikālaghu is as sad as I am." He came near the spring. The blue horse, a manifestation of Hayagrīva, said to the man, "That girl, who has accumulated merits in her previous life, has invoked Hayagrīva for these five months. This you could not do in five long years. If you wish to return to your place, mount me, the best of the stallions and never look back." The man was overjoyed, he mounted the horse and instantly reached home.

Then thousands of red soldiers on horses from the place of the local ghosts chased him and arrived at the fortress gate. In their midst was a red man, as big as a mountain with the head of a scorpion. The youngest daughter visualized Hayagrīva on her crown, generated compassion and said, "You accumulated bad karma in your previous lives, so you are born with a scorpion head. What a pity that you will be crushed under stones of hell until the end of Saṁsāra." Then, all at once, everything disappeared. While others cannot see anything, the deer antler enabled her to see everything. The girl returned to her room and saw that the prince was there. She was overjoyed and jumped to embrace him. The mother also saw him and fainted. All members of the family saw the return of the prince and paid their respect. Everybody cried out in joy. To welcome their prince, they offered prayers and held grand festivities.

That youngest daughter gave birth to three princes and three princesses. Due to the power of her merits, the kingdom thrived with joy and happiness. As the kingdom had no other princes, the prince and the youngest daughter ruled the kingdom, whose wealth and prosperity equaled to heavenly mansions. The prince and the youngest daughter ruled day and night according to the Dharma and lived happily ever after.

Then Prince Gautamiputra remarked, "How lucky that the youngest daughter was enthusiastic and determined to accomplish the Hayagrīva meditation." The Siddhivad corpse cried, "The corpse now got a reply!" The Siddhivad corpse slapped the prince three times and disappeared.

Here ends the twenty-eighth Siddhivad corpse story, Lady Kaphalikālaghu.

1. Tib. Rta mgrin (Skt. Hayagrīva) literally meaning horse-throat, is a wrathful manifestation of Lord Avalokiteśvara.
2. Tib. Bya pho mtshal lu (Skt. Kukkutahingula), means the rooster.
3. Tib. Sla nga slang chung (Skt. Kaphalikālaghu), means small iron pan.

29 The Kind Horse

Once again, Prince Gautamiputra walked towards the tree to catch the corpse. The prince shouted, "Are you coming down, or do I cut down this tree?" The corpse climbed down. The prince then tied the neck and the arms of the corpse together and the legs were tied tightly with the magical rope and the corpse was forced into the magical bag. Then the prince began his journey. When he had barely taken seven steps, the corpse said, "Oh prince, just say something." Knowing what the corpse wanted, the prince kept silent. Then the Siddhivad corpse said, "The unfortunate prince doesn't speak. Now, listen to me and I'll tell you a short story, as short as the width of a buckwheat."

The Siddhivad corpse then narrated the following story:

Once in a vast valley lived an old couple and their very good tempered daughter. The daughter took refuge in the Three Jewels[1] and observed proper religious practices. The mother arranged all of her needs and necessities for her.

One day, a demon decided to ask for the daughter's hand in marriage. Disguised as a young man, he put on a white wool robe. Then wielding a bow in his hand, he appeared at the door of the house. Then he asked, "Give me your daughter." The old couple said, "If you could tell me her name, we would surely give her to you. But until then, we cannot part with her." The demon then left their place.

The next day, the demon came carrying a carcass of horse on his right shoulder and a human corpse on his left. Gripping the corpse of a child in his mouth, he was rolling a ball of yarn. A fox came running up near him and said, "Brother Demon, please give me some meat." The demon said, "I can give you meat, only if you tell me the name of the old couple's daughter that lives in the lower part of the valley. I'll give you lots of meat."

The fox went to the lower valley and eavesdropped at their home to find the name of the old couple's daughter, but could hear nothing throughout the night. The next morning, the mother called out, "Daughter, Sokdadilī,[2] come and get dressed." The fox heard this and said, "Yelp, I now have the daughter's name" and the fox then returned to the demon's place. The demon was waiting for the fox. As the fox was close to the demon, it jumped and slipped. In the fall, the fox lost its concentration and forgot her name. The fox scurried back and forth with its mouth wide open. The demon called out, "Come here. What are you doing there?" The fox said, "I knew her name, but I forgot it on my way here." The demon said, "Anyway, eat some meat and go again to old couple's house and listen more closely."

Once again, the fox went to the old couple's house and hid among the logs and eavesdropped on them. The fox could hear nothing during the night. However, at sunrise, the old mother called out, "Daughter Sokdadilī, rise and get dressed." The fox, fearing that it would forget her name, continuously repeated her name "Sokdadilī" as it traveled to the demon's place. The demon was waiting at the upper part of the ravine. The fox arrived there repeating her name. Finally, the fox said to the demon, "Her name is Sokdadilī."

The demon took a lot of gold and turquoise gems and went to the old couple's house to ask for the girl. The demon gave all the gold and turquoise gems to the old couple and said, "Give me your daughter." They were pleased for the gold and turquoise gems and said, "If you could tell us our daughter's name, we will give her to you. Otherwise, we shall not." The demon replied, "Her name is Sokdadilī." The old couple said, "That's right. You can have her now." However, the old couple were very sad. Then looking at her the demon beckoned, "Come, come with me." The old couple said, "How can you take her without a horse?" The demon replied, "You didn't ask me to bring a horse. Now, we will travel by foot." However, the old couple said, "We would like the gift of a horse for our daughter." The demon refused to accept this saying, "I don't want a horse unless you let me ride on the same horse." The daughter said, "Let us do as my parents say." Then she prepared to go. As she went up to an intelligent horse, it cautioned her, "Better go with him this time. Even if you tried to stay, the demon will eat you. Tie these seven grains of barley around your neck. One day, you may need them. If you scatter these grains, it will help you escape. But you should go at least this one time." Then the demon left the old couple's house and the daughter followed him.

When the demon and daughter reached the lower valley, he rode on something resembling a sheep's head and beckoned, "Come, ride with me." The daughter was helpless and rode with him. There were three roads and he followed the long and narrow one. They came to a nine-storey iron fortress that was as tall as the sky. When they entered the fortress, there were treasures of wealth and storehouses of food and drink. The demon would go out every morning. One day the girl said, "You went out every day and I feel very lonely." One day, the demon left a puppy and a piece of food. The puppy ate the food, but in the evening, the food ate the puppy. Then the next day, the goat ate a bunch of grass, while in the evening, the grass ate the goat. She thought this is an indication of the impermanent nature of our existence.

Then one day, the demon left a bunch of keys with the daughter. They were magical keys and could miraculously open any door. The keys also enabled her to see the outside world like frozen water in the cold winter, people plowing their fields, the crops ripening, workers weeding their fields, women harvesting crops. She could see many other things too. However, there was a filthy black door, which the key could not open. The daughter drank something that tasted delicious and lied down flat on the ground. Then her eyes saw there was a key between the beams. She took the key and opened the filthy black door. In the right corner of the room, there was an old sluggish woman and to her left, there were many women lying and gasping for air. The old woman said, "Has a fortunate woman come by here?" The daughter asked, "Why do you say this?" The old woman replied, "When young, we too were treated well. We have all been his

wives at one time, but you can see what happens when you become old. Do you see these corpses? You will be just like them." The daughter said, "Is there any thing I can do to avert this?" The old woman said, "You are lucky to have the keys. The demon had not trusted us with the keys. Now, take the gold and turquoise gems from that old corpse. Skin her head and wear it on yours. Put on her remaining skin, wear her worn out clothes and put on her gold and turquoise gems too. Then go straight to the lower valley, where a religious king rules. Go, to see him." The daughter was pleased and very thankful. She put on the old woman's skin and wore her tattered clothes. She then dressed up herself with the gold and turquoise gems. Having securely locked the door, she walked down towards the lower valley.

When the demon returned to the fortress, he could not find the girl. He then rode on the sheep-head and began to search for her. In barely a moment or so, he found the girl, now disguised as an old woman. He asked, "Old lady, have you seen a girl walk down this road?" She replied, "I didn't see anyone go by." She was so frightened that she collapsed to the ground. As she fell, he heard some metallic sound. He asked, "What is that metallic sound that I hear?" She said, "That was the cracking sound of my old bones." He turned away, but again he heard another metallic sound. He again said, "What is that?" She said, "It might be the cracking of a yet another old bone."

Having met the demon three times on her way, the girl finally hid herself in the king's field. The field caretakers shouted from the top of the fortress, but she couldn't hear anything. He came down near to her and she saw an old woman with her walking stick. He asked, "Old woman, where do you come from?" She replied, "I came from the upper valley. Can I get a job to fetch water, parch grains for flour and do other chores?" He said, "Would it be possible for you to fetch water and parch barley?" She replied, "To save myself from the cold and hunger, I have no choice but to work." He said, "If you can, we need one worker." Then he took her to the palace and she started fetching water and sweeping floors inside the palace.

One day, while the old woman went to fetch water, a stableman was bringing his horses to water. He was shocked, the stable keeper saw that she has taken off her skin cover and hung it on a tree. He saw a very beautiful girl with many layers of turquoise gems and gold ornaments. He quickly ran to the palace and informed this to the king. The king said, "Let her come here. We shall then ask why she cheated on us." As she appeared in the palace, the stableman and a few other servants pretended to tease and push the old woman around. They tugged at her worn out clothes and they ripped her old woman skin into pieces. When the king arrived there, he saw a very beautiful girl. The king asked, "Why did you disguise yourself in that horrible form?" She recounted the whole story and said, "I would prefer that I be allowed to wear the old woman's skin for two more days." The king said, "You stay in here. The demon of the land can't harm you." She requested, "Please, keep the doors closed."

Then the daughter became the queen. As the years passed, she became pregnant. Before the birth of the child, the king left with his ministers and attendants for summer camping. During his absence, the queen gave birth to a prince, whose upper body was of gold, his lower body of silver, his waist of a white conch shell and his eyebrows of turquoise gems. The ministers and subjects were very happy with the newborn prince and they sent a message to the king.

It read:

> Our queen has given birth to an extraordinary prince with an upper body of gold, a lower body of silver, a waistline of a white conch shell and sparkling eyebrows of turquoise gems We hope everything is fine with you. Oh king, return soon.

The messenger climbed up to the high mountain pass. Near the top of the pass, the demon was spinning and twirling yarn. The demon asked, "How are you?" He replied, "Fine sir, how are you?" The demon then asked, "Where are you going?" He said, "I am going to inform our king of the birth of an extraordinary prince born to our queen, Sokdadilī." The demon said, "You have been running, you must be hungry. Eat to your satisfaction." He gave bread to the messenger. While the messenger was eating, the demon re-wrote the letter.

The forged letter read:

> Your majesty, this is a humble prayer from your subjects. Our queen has given birth to a prince with the head of a monkey and the body of a donkey. This being a bad omen, we know not what to do.

Then the messenger went and delivered the letter to the king.

The king wrote a reply that read:

> My dear ministers and subjects, whatever the form of the prince that was born to our queen, make sure that every care is taken until my return.

When the messenger was on his way back, he met the demon again, who again changed the letter.

It now read:

> All men must come with weapons and all women with loads of dust. When I ride through the pass, I must not see that son of mine.

As the messenger returned to the kingdom and the letter was read out, the women shouted, "We should remove this queen" and all the subjects were disappointed. However, the king's order can't be disobeyed. They let the queen ride a red donkey with a white spot on its forehead, then all the people chased the queen out and expelled her to the back of the mountain pass.

As the queen reached on the pass, the demon was already there and he said, "Oh girl, you are here." She replied, "Yes, I have come." The demon said, "Show me the evil son." The demon took the child in his hands and said, "Never before did I manage to get such nice food." Then he swallowed the son. The demon gave some meat to her saying, "Eat this, you must be hungry." Then the demon said, "You had a son with the upper body of gold, because you stole my gold. Your son's lower body was silver, because you stole my silver. His waist was a conch shell, because love to you was as pure as a conch shell. His eyebrows were turquoise gems, because I have been watching you all these years. I have something for you to eat, but first check for fleas on my head. What a pity!" The queen kept on looking for fleas on his head. Then she thought that nothing could go as bad as this. The queen took the seven grains of barley from her neck. She scattered them around and cried, "My intelligent horse!" Instantly, the horse miraculously appeared before her. She slowly covered his head with a cloth, rode the horse and fled. The demon went inside the hut to get a horse. However, by that time, the horse and the girl were far from his sight.

The queen arrived at a strange place far off. She wept and endured a heavy snowstorm. The horse said, "If you weep, you will die due to the freezing temperature. If you skin me and wear my carcass, you will be warm and there will be sunshine very soon." Again, the horse said, "After skinning me, spread it here. Take out the brain and scatter it around the rocks on this mountain pass. Pluck my hairs and scatter them on the mountain. Place my head in the center of the skin and place my heart and two kidneys alongside. Place my four limbs upright at the four corners. Surround the skin by the intestines and keep the two eyes under the skin and hide the heart and the liver underneath the skin." Then the horse neighed loudly and died.

The queen wept and there was a heavy rain and snow. She then stopped crying and skinned the horse. Then there was warm sunshine. She did what the horse told her to do. Having worked hard, she was tired and felt asleep. After a while, she was awakened from sleep by the loud barking of a dog. She suddenly got up and saw snow capped mountains and waterfalls in the upper valley. There were rows of fields in the lower valley, while the middle valley was filled with a lush green pasture that looked like a tray full of turquoise gems. There she saw a square shaped castle. Its base stood firm on the ground and its towers almost pierced the sky. Layers of fenced walls with four watchtowers in the four directions were protecting the castle. As she entered, there were many people living there and everyone said, "Welcome, queen."

The horse's kidneys turned into dogs that waited for her at the gates. The heart had turned into a beautiful horse that stood waiting outside the door. The two eyes had turned into two fresh springs on the either side of the city. The lung and liver had turned into stacks of meat, butter and other edible food. From the bile inside the carcass flowed an enormous amount of gold and turquoise gems. The horse's stomach that was spread out had now become the lush green meadows. The horse's brain scattered on the rocks had become the snow capped mountains, which appeared like pillars supporting the vast expanse of the sky. The horse's hairs scattered over the mountains became a rich forest.

The daughter became the queen of the kingdom and lived happily for three years. Then she tried to search for her husband, the king. One day, while she was walking on the roof of the fort, she saw many horsemen coming from the same path which she traversed. She watched carefully and recognized the king. She ran and jumped down the steps from the roof. When the king arrived at the gate, she was overjoyed and embraced him. The king too shed tears and embraced her. She told the whole story to the king. The king said, "You are right, don't be sad." The ministers said to the king, "The messenger was an unworthy person. The queen is truly innocent." Then she invited the king into the fort and served him everything. The king asked, "Is this your parents' home?" She said, "I was fortunate enough to see my parents, but I got all these through the kindness of my intelligent horse." The king said, "You had no horse when you came to my place. Where did you get a horse?" She told the above story and the king was delighted. The king said, "That intelligent horse has been kinder than even your real parents."

Then the king and the queen ruled over the two kingdoms in accordance with the Dharma and the subjects became as prosperous and happy as they could be.

Prince Gautamiputra then remarked, "The horse had been very kind to the girl." The corpse said, "The corpse finally got a reply." The Siddhivad corpse slapped the prince three times and disappeared like before. The prince wondered, "How careless of me to forget the advice of my master Nāgārjuna!"

Here ends the twenty-ninth Siddhivad corpse, The Kind Horse.

1. Tib. Dkon mchog gsum, literally means three jewels. It refers to the three ultimate objects of refuge in Buddhism, the Buddha, his teachings and his disciples.

2. Tib. Sokha' dili (Skt. Sokdadilī)

30 The Girl Who Exchanged Pleasure for Pain

Once again, Prince Gautamiputra returned to Śītavana cemetery. As the prince beat the corpse with a hoe, the corpse cried "Aah! Laa!" As the prince bound the corpse with the magical rope and forced the corpse into the magical bag, the corpse cried, "Ooh! Loo!" Then the prince started his journey as before. The corpse shouted, "Prince, prince! Either you tell me a story or I'll tell you one." Knowing what the corpse wanted, the prince remained silent. The Siddhivad corpse then said, "The prince can only listen and can't talk."

The Siddhivad corpse then narrated the following story:

Once, there was a king, who ruled over the lower portion of a valley. In the upper valley, there lived an old woman and her daughter who had as neighbors, a witch mother and her daughter.

One day, the old woman's daughter went to the witch mother and daughter to get some fire. They offered her a human ear lightly roasted with grain and mustard seeds. She found it very tasty. The witch and her daughter asked, "Would you like to come to my house?" The old woman's daughter said, "I want to, but my mother would never allow that." "Then why don't you kill your mother and come live with us," said the witch. The old woman's daughter then asked, "How do I kill my mother?" The witch mother said, "Just pretend that you are ill and your mother will ask you for a remedy. Tell her that there is a way, but it is impossible to accomplish. When your mother persuades you, tell her that you'll have to hold the upper grinding stone, while she sweeps the surface of the lower grinder with both her breasts. If she does that, she will certainly cure your sickness." The old woman's daughter returned home and did what she was told to do. Her mother said to her, "If this could cure you, then I shall certainly do that. Now hold the grinder over my breasts and lift it up." The old woman's daughter did what she was told and while her mother cleaned the surface of the lower grinding stone with her breasts, the daughter let go off the upper grinding stone, which crushed her mother's breasts and killed her.

The old woman's daughter then called the witch, "Come to my house. I have killed my mother." The witch mother and daughter came to the old woman's house. They fed on her mother's flesh and gnawed on her bones. They took all the meat, butter from her house, leaving only the vegetables and some left over juice from squeezed grains fermented to make wine. They sent her to collect wood and herd their cattle. They let her wear only the old clothes, while they put on the nice new clothes.

The old woman's daughter collected ten loads of wood every day. She was sad and lonely. Her deceased mother could not bear this and thus took a rebirth in the form of the witches' cow and gave them milk and butter. After a few days, the cow said to her daughter, "My daughter, who exchanged pleasure for pain. Evening is drawing to a close, take home a bigger load of wood than before and you shall get warm food."

One day, the witch mother said, "I feed my own daughter with meat and butter and give you only the wine residue. But how come you are healthier?" The old woman's daughter was afraid that if she told the truth, the demon would slaughter the cow. So, she said, "Our red cow used to address me as 'the daughter who exchanged pleasure for pain' and spread my robes for bed sheets to sleep on. I slept in my robes, spun wool and collected wood. That's how I remain happy and healthy." The witch mother said, "Why didn't you tell this before? I am sending my own daughter to herd the cattle. Stay away from my cattle, you beggar." Then the witch mother sent her daughter to look after the cattle. The cow said, "Oh daughter, who exchanged pleasure for pain. Spread your robe and sleep on it." When the witch's daughter woke up, she found dung on her robe. The yarn entangled everywhere on the trees and the cattle had strayed

across the valley. She could not return home until dusk. When the witch mother asked, "My daughter, why were you so late?" The witch's daughter replied, "I dozed off after spreading my robe. When I woke up, the cattle was all over the place and the woolen yarn was entangled all over the trees." The witch mother and her daughter decided to kill the cow, which was in fact their old neighbor. The cow said to her daughter, "Tell them, what meat you should get is for them to decide. Then whatever meat you get, bury it under the stairs." She did this.

One day, the witch mother and her daughter were informed about a fair in the lower valley. Both of them dressed themselves in their best clothes and put on their ornaments. They mixed barley and mustard seeds from two pots and asked the old woman's daughter, "Separate the barley from the mustard. Finish by the time we return, or we will kill you." Then they left.

After a while, a pigeon came to her and said, "Oh my daughter, who exchanged pleasure for pain. Dress up well, tie your sash, put on gold and silver ornaments and go to the fair to watch the show." The cow's skin had turned into clothes, the four limbs had turned into a pair of shoes, the intestines changed into a sash and the flesh into gold, turquoise gems and coral ornaments. The old woman's daughter put on the dress and wore a pair of shoes and the ornaments. Then she returned and requested that the pigeon help her to separate the barley and mustard seeds.

As the old woman's daughter arrived at the market and walked around, she saw a handsome king. In the market, she also saw the witch mother and her daughter buying food. Then, she hurried back home, jumping over a shallow stream. One of her shoes fell into the stream. When she reached home, she hid her clothes and ornaments in the ground. She found that the pigeon had already separated the barley from the mustard seeds. One of the king's horses refused to drink water and ran away. When the stable keeper followed the horse, he found the horse sniffing at the shoe in the stream. He took the shoe and informed the king. The king said, "Yesterday, I saw a young lady, about fifteen years old, with the signs of ḍākinī. Today my intelligent horse found a trace of her. We should search for this lady and make her my queen." When the witch mother and daughter returned to their house, the old woman's daughter said, "Welcome, who was the best looking man and the best woman at the fair today? As for the dres[1] of barley and mustard seed, I have already separated them." The witch mother shouted, "Shut up, who do you think you are?"

Again, the next day, the witch mother and daughter put on their best dress and ornaments and left for the market. In the market, a minister called aloud, "Where is the well dressed young lady, whose shoe we found yesterday? Show yourself!" No girl responded to the minister. The witch's daughter came up to the minister and tried on the shoe. However, the shoe would not fit her and her toes were injured. Then, the old woman's daughter came up to the minister, took off her two shoes and hung them on her shoulder. Saying, "This shoe will fit only me. And I have the other one here." The witch daughter asked, "Does she not look like the girl who lives with us?" The witch mother said, "Yes, how can she be so lucky?" Then the old woman's daughter was taken as the queen. The witch mother and daughter returned home and found many footprints and the excrement of birds around. They have eaten all the grains as well. The witch mother thought, "That girl's mother must have been born as a pigeon. Only she could have done this."

The old woman's daughter, now the queen, soon gave birth to a prince named Siddhārth.[2] From the time of his birth, the kingdom became very prosperous. One day, the witch daughter came to the palace and said, "I came to see my sister. Please, forgive what I did to her." Just by way of teasing, the witch daughter asked the queen, "What do you serve the king? What do you give to your servants?" The queen casually replied, "I serve milk porridge to the king and all kinds of delicious food to the servants." The witch daughter then asked the queen, "What food do you give to the horse, Rukmavati[3] and the white dog?" The queen said, "I give plants, leaves, stalks, and grain like corn to the horse and bones to the white dog." The witch daughter asked, "How do you look after prince Siddhārth and conduct yourself in the palace?" The queen said, "Prince Siddhārth is not very close to me. Every time I pass by, I slap him and I give him a bad look. Also, when I walk up or down the stairs, I stomp hard on the steps." Then after a while, the witch daughter said, "Sister, you must wash your hair. I will help you. As you are the queen, let us go to the pool and bathe together." As they arrived at the lake, the queen took off her ornaments and clothes. As she bent down to wash her hair, the witch daughter pushed her into the water. Then the witch daughter put on the queen's dress and ornaments and then entered the palace. She conducted herself the same way the queen did. She treated the horse, dog, prince, the king and the subjects as the queen had explained to her and she prepared food suitable for donkeys. When the subjects came everyday for fire, they asked each other if the queen had gone mad.

Suddenly, one day the horse Rukmavati refused to drink water. The horse ran from the lake shore and shed tears. A golden bird appeared from the middle of the lake and landed on a tree, it said, "Oh king! Which queen has served you better, the previous one or this one? Who takes more care of Prince Siddhārth? Who gives better treatment to the horses and the attendants and the subjects? Why was this small bird pushed into water?" Then the bird disappeared from the water. The stableman quickly returned to the palace and informed the king, "The horse Rukmavati refused to drink water and ran away. It neighed and shed tears. A golden bird with a turquoise crest landed on the tree and asked many questions." The king said, "Let's go and see tomorrow. I had bad dreams and the queen's behavior had changed." The king returned to the lake with the stableman. At the lake, the bird repeated what he had told the stableman the previous day. The king shed tears and asked, "Come here, my bird." The bird landed on the king's palm and again repeated the same story. The king caught hold of the bird, but the bird cried, "It was my mistake. Please, let me go." It pleaded three times. The king asked, "If there's a solution, tell me." The bird said, "You are being deceived. The current queen is a witch's daughter. She took me

to the lake and drowned me in the water. But, there may be a way." The king insisted to know the method from the bird. The bird then said, "Now you go to the palace and talk to no one about this incident. Wrap me in various colors of silk and keep me in the treasure room. Then let many Bon[4] priests perform rites for longevity and prosperity for seven days. Ask the queen to ferment a lot of wine. Dig out a deep ditch under her place that just fits her size, spread a cloth mattress on it and make her sit there. After she falls in the ditch, she will surely die of suffocation. Then I will be revived to life and I can live with you." The king and the ministers were very pleased and did everything accordingly. The witch daughter tumbled into the ditch as she sat on the mattress.

When the witch daughter was dead, the king, the ministers and the subjects went into the treasury room and found the queen alive again. The king told his subjects, "Cut off the witch daughter's head and roll the head inside a big ball of yarn, as big as a pitcher." Then the king arranged for all sorts of delicious food. He loaded them on his horse Rukmavati and sent the queen to visit the witch mother. The queen went to the witch's house and served all the delicious foods she brought with her. She asked, "Mother, have you been well?" The witch mother replied, "No, I have not been well. Were you able to deceive the queen? Did the king notice you? You now seem to look more like the old mother's daughter." The queen then fixed a piece of red cloth on the upper window. Then she came down and said to the witch mother, "I must go to the palace now. The king might scold me. Please unwind this ball of thread for me, as I am leaving." The witch mother advised her, "You should keep in mind that the king must not know how to treat his subjects and look after prince Siddhārth."

The queen promised that she would do as she was told. Then the witch mother brought a long thread holder staff and started unwinding the thread ball. The queen quickly mounted the horse and escaped. The witch mother continued unwinding the thread ball, after a while she saw an ear. As she looked further, she saw that her daughter's head was within the ball. At once, the witch mother ran after her. When she was about to catch her, the queen said, "Old witch, your house is on fire. Do you still want to follow me? My horse being swift, you can't get hold of me." As the witch mother looked back, she saw the red cloth flashing on her window, which she thought was fire and she turned back.

Then the queen arrived at the palace. Thus, she was able to take revenge on the witch mother and her daughter. The king ruled the kingdom according to the Dharma and the subjects enjoyed great prosperity and happiness.

Prince Gautamiputra said, "She could have been happier if her mother was alive. Both the mother and the daughter being ḍākinīs, they were able to subdue the witch mother and daughter. Fortunately, she finally became the queen." The corpse said, "You finally talked to this corpse." The Siddhivad corpse slapped the prince three times and flew away like a dart.

Here ends the thirtieth Siddhivad corpse story, The Girl Who Exchanged Pleasure for Pain.

1. Tib. Dre (bre) a unit of volume equiv. to 250 ml, and approx. weighing 250 g. They are normally made of wood and used to measure grains and other dry commodities.
2. Tib. Don grub (Skt. Siddhārth), literally means accomplished one.
3. Tib. Gser ldan (Skt. Rukmavati), literally means golden-hued.
4. A religion supposedly pre-dating Buddhism in terms of its advent in Tibet, and is still followed by a considerable number of Tibetans.

31 The Kingdom Founded on a Trade Route

The Siddhivad corpse said, "Such an unfortunate prince like you would not talk to me. Anyway, listen and I'll tell you a story."

The Siddhivad corpse then narrated the following story:

Once upon a time, there lived a mighty king who ruled over a vast kingdom. Among his subjects, there was a rich elderly couple and their only son. The old father performed religious practices all day and night. The old mother, being very wise, looked after all the other chores. All the neighbors loved the old mother very much.

One day, many traders of that kingdom were preparing to leave on a trade mission. They played a joke on the old man's son and said to him, "Why not try your luck in business? You could have inexhaustible wealth." The son said to his old parents, "I would like to go on the trade mission." However, the old parents said, "Our family never engaged in trade and we are still rich. So, you should not do business." The son urged his old mother, "I want to go with them." The old mother said, "We have never been traders. Our ancestors were kind hearted and truthful folks. Abstaining from causing any harm or loss to anybody, this is the good Dharma way of life. We are having a happy life now. Also, that you being my only son, I can't let you go." Yet, the son insistently said, "If you don't let me go on the trade mission, I'll run away."

The old mother told this to the old father. The old father summoned his son and said, "You have everything you need for this life. I would rather send you to gather merits, as it benefits you in your future lives. If you take up business, you will waste this precious life in doing a business. Don't go for trade, my son." The son said, "If you do not let me go, I will do business elsewhere, I'll run away."

The old parents discussed that if he escaped, it would bring a bad name to their family. It was better to let him go on the trade mission. Though the old father was reluctant, the old mother said, "He is determined to go, let him go. He will see the outside world and gain some experience." The old father said, "Our neighbors are good people. He may see far-away places and gain new knowledge and experiences, but in the process we may lose our only son, especially when we are old." The old mother said, "He is not willing to live here anymore, so I hope nothing bad will happen to him." They decided to let him go on the trade mission and made all the arrangements for the business trip.

Then their only son left with the other traders. After traveling about fifteen days, they arrived at a big market-place. There, the son found a host and stayed alone. However, the other traders left him behind. The host asked, "Where are your fellow traders?" He replied, "They have all left." The host said, "It is very difficult to go all alone from here. Better wait till they return." He said, "I did not actually come here to trade and accumulate wealth. Despite my parents' reluctance, I just followed them." The host said, "If you really want to go, then take this sword with you and never ever part with this. To the enemies with physical form, just display this sword and you need not even strike. For formless ghosts, you don't even need to draw it out." Thus, the host gave him the sword.

The son tied the sword around his waist, loaded up his animals and followed the footprints of the traders that he was traveling with. Then he reached a big valley at sunset and he could not trace their footprints anymore. Then he saw many big houses and finally arrived at the gate of a palace. He found the main gate open and entered the palace. There was not a single person visible. All the cattle were about to die without grass and water in the cattle shed. He then checked the spacious stables and saw that all the horses were about to die also from lack of livestock

food and water. Moreover, he saw nobody there. He kept his animals in the corner and climbed the stairs of the palace. As he arrived in the middle room, all the attendants and the ministers were lying dead. The king was dead on a golden throne and the queen was dead on a turquoise throne. Still he could not find anybody there. He gave plenty of livestock food to the horses and lots of grass to the cattle. He kept his animals in a corner and provided them with plenty of grass and water too.

One by one, the son closed all the doors and blocked them with stones. He then piled the dead bodies on the golden and turquoise throne. There was a wealth of meat and wine to eat. He took a big vase of wine and a full portion of meat. He made a big bonfire and drank a lot of wine. Enjoying the meat, he stayed there that evening.

At about midnight, the door suddenly burst open. The son placed a hand on the handle of the sword and sat there with a relaxed mind. Then he mumbled to himself, "An enemy with form can be defeated only by drawing out this sword. For formless ghosts, I don't even need to draw the sword." There was a stepping sound of someone climbing up stairs. Then he saw a monstrous monkey on top of the staircase. It has a long tail and had many decorations on its shoulder. A few moments later, six monkeys arrived noisily chattering. They walked around him three times and they also walked around a big black box three times that was there. Then resting their heads on the wood of the box, they sat there yawning and feeling sleepy..

As dawn came, the sword moved back down into its sheath. The monkeys were not there. When the sun rose, the son decided to leave the place. He walked downstairs, but found all the doors locked. He gave grass, water and livestock food to the horses and cattle like before. Then he went back and sat at the same place. He made a fire, drank wine, and ate roasted flour and meat.

At midnight, there was a loud knock and the door opened. A monkey, but not the same as the last night, came in with a skull and a ritual dagger[1] in its hand. The monkey, one of the biggest he had ever seen, wore a small cap on his head. Then there appeared seven monkeys holding skulls and ritual daggers, followed by more monkeys playing drums and other musical instruments. His sword shook a bit. Then the monkey started dancing. He could not control his sword and it moved up about a hands width[2] from its sheath. The monkeys cried "chatter, chatter..." and looked at one another with eyes wide open. One by one, the monkeys climbed down the stairs. That night he ate meat, drank wine and stayed there.

The next morning at sunrise, the son went down and again found all the doors closed as before. Again, he gave grass and water to the horses and cattle and stayed inside. Now he could hear human voices near the door. He thought that last night there were no people and he wondered who they could be. As he looked, he saw two exorcists wearing black hats. He walked up to them with the sword. The exorcists greeted him, "Hello." He replied, "Hello." The exorcists said, "Let us in." He said, "That's right, if there is anything to discuss, let us do it inside." As soon as the two exorcists entered the palace, he closed the door. The exorcists said, "Don't close the door. Formless ghosts can not harm you. You can bring in more humans, as they are afraid of your sword and soon will flee." Then, he kept the door open and went inside.

The son promised that he would not draw the sword out and that the exorcists would not harm him. He served wine and various kinds of foods to them. He asked, "Why are all these people dead?" They said, "Our guardian deity was displeased. The king and queen entrusted us to be their priests. We had gift of armor by our guardian deity and it was more precious than a wish fulfilling jewel. Once, we had no grains to eat. We borrowed grain from the king and left the armor as collateral. Later we paid for the grains and requested our armor back, but the king refused. Therefore, the guardian deity became angry and killed the king and all of his staff using his magic power. You have been truly fortunate. Your sword seems restless and about to spring out of the sheath by itself. You can be the king of this kingdom and let us be your priests. Our armor is in that black box. Please give it to us." The son said, "I'll give you the armor, but you have to be my

priests for many generations to come." The exorcists informed the people, "Our previous king had become a ghost and we now have a Dharma king." The people appealed to the son, "Please be our king and we will serve you well." Then the son became the king, and he enjoyed a very happy royal life.

Later, some traders arrived at the palace to seek food. As the king watched from his palace, he recognized that the traders were from his hometown. The king asked his servant, "Bring those traders here." The traders thought, "We don't know this king. Maybe he wishes to give us trouble and they stayed away." The servant informed the king, "The traders refused to come. So they are going away." The king again sent a servant to summon them. The servant told the traders, "Our king is your colleague you left behind at the market place. He insists that you take as much grass and livestock food as you may need. So, come to the palace." The traders were pleased and eagerly entered the palace. They were all surprised to see the king and were awe-struck. The king served them delicious food and drinks and they stayed for a few days. They offered an elephant load of gold and silver to the king.

The king then sent a trusted minister with many horsemen to escort his parents to the palace. He also sent away his friends with many horses, armor, etc. The traders returned home to their place and told the story about the king. The minister conveyed the king's message to his old parents.

The king of the kingdom where the old parents lived, wondered, "How could a son of these old couple conquer other kingdom and take his parents away?" The king asked his ministers, "Is that kingdom powerful and wealthy?" They told the king that the kingdom that is ruled by the old couple's son was very powerful. Therefore, the king let his parents go there with the ministers. He also gave away his princess and ten elephant loads of gifts. The parents arrived in his kingdom with the princess. His old parents and the princess saw the successful and flourishing kingdom and were pleased. Then the king sent a minister to the market place to search for the kind host, who gave him the sword as a gift. The minister brought the host to the king's palace. The king treated him to a grand royal event at the palace.

Then Prince Gautamiputra remarked, "The son was very fortunate and his host was very kind indeed." The Siddhivad corpse said, "You finally spoke to the corpse." Then, the Siddhivad corpse disappeared once again.

Here ends the thirty-first Siddhivad corpse story, The Kingdom Founded on a Trade Route.

1. Tib. Phur ba (Skt. Kīla) is a three-sided knife, shaped like a dagger, used in tantric rituals.
2. Tib. Mtho gang, a measurement equal to the length from the tip of the thumb to the tip of middle finger in an extended palm.

32 The Fortunate Man

Once again, Prince Gautamiputra walked to Śītavana cemetery. Standing at the foot of a tree, the prince shouted, "Oh corpse, either you come down or I will cut this old tree." The Siddhivad corpse slowly climbed down. Prince Gautamiputra tied the corpse with a rope and forced the corpse into a sack. Then carrying the sack on his back, the prince began his journey. After he had barely taken seven steps, the corpse said, "Oh prince, you look so upset." The prince was very angry and did not say anything. The corpse said, "I know, a prince like you would never talk. Listen, I will tell you a very short story."

The Siddhivad corpse then narrated the following story:

Once, there was a great king, who ruled over a kingdom in the upper part of a valley. The valley had rows of fertile fields and a huge lake that watered the fields. Two Nāgas, who were the custodian of the lake, lived there. They ate whoever came to the lake to release water for irrigation. Therefore, the villagers rolled a dice to decide who should risk meeting the Nāgas when they went to release water from the lake.

One day, they rolled the dice and it was the prince's turn to go and release water for the fields. Both the king and the queen were sad. In the same kingdom was a poor elderly couple, who lived with their son. The prince was very kind to him. The elderly couple's son went to the palace and said to the king and the queen, "Please, don't be sad. Let the prince stay and I will go in his place. Doing this, we can save the royal lineage. Please, don't forget to conduct the necessary rites after my death, so that your subjects may not speak lowly of your kingship. If I die, provide food and drink to my old parents. Although I feel sad, let me go to the lake." Then the elderly couple's son carried all the provisions arranged for him and a shovel too. As he arrived near the lake, he released water for the fields below. Then thinking he should die for the prince, slept nearby. However, no one came to eat him that day.

The next morning after sunrise, the poor couple's son looked around and saw a black snake and a tortoise yelling at each other. The tortoise said, "He was sleeping right here, you missed him." The snake replied, "You are wrong, if you had come a little earlier, he was just here." Then the tortoise said, "You are wrong, if you had eaten the man last night, it would have been fine." Then the tortoise shouted, "You beggar, lowly snake! You careless creature! If somebody washed you and ate you, even his vomit would turn to gold." The snake said, "You should be killed and your carcass should be wrapped in five colors of silk and kept in the royal treasure room." They argued and were blaming each other and then they started fighting. The poor couple's son used this opportunity to hit their heads with the shovel and kill them. He wondered if what they said could come true. He washed the snake with water and swallowed it. He forced himself to vomit and fantastically, it changed into gold. Then he took the skin of the tortoise and wrapped it with five colors of silk and took the tortoise skin to the king's palace.

Then as the poor couple's son returned home, he saw his parents observing an elaborate post funeral rite. The people treated his old parents very well. Seeing the son unexpectedly return home, the people around him asked, "How did you manage to return? We received the most amount of water this year and everybody is happy. Even if the king himself passes away, we couldn't have observed a better post funeral rite." All were happy and all embraced him. The poor couple's son said, "I feel good that I could return." The poor couple's son went to the palace to see the king, the queen and the prince. They all embraced him and asked, "It is nice that you have come. How did you return? How did this happen? This year we got an abundant amount of water." He replied, "It is through the grace of your highness and the time of my death has not yet come. Last night, I went to the lake to release water from the lake. However, no one came to eat me. The next morning as I woke up from my sleep, I saw a tortoise and a snake fighting. The tortoise said to the snake, "If you were killed, washed and swallowed by a person, the vomit of that person would instantly turn into gold." The snake said, "If you are killed, wrapped in five colors of silk and stored in the treasure room, your carcass would be as precious as the priceless jewels there." Then they started fighting. By afternoon, I killed them both with my shovel. Now the snake and the tortoise from the lake are no more. In the future there is no need to roll a dice to see who will release water from the lake. I offer you the precious golden tortoise to your highness."

Thereafter, the king treated him like his own son. After sometime, the king and the queen passed away and the elderly couple died as well. The poor couple's son hosted a fifteen-day public feast for the sake of his parents. He sculpted statues and printed Buddhist scriptures for the sake of his deceased parents and he placed them in the container for religious relics in a Stūpa.

One day, the prince, now enthroned as the king, said to the elderly couple's son, "Let us go for a walk." They took along some bread and a bow and arrows. They crossed eighteen mountain passes and valleys and crossed high mountains. They saw many people gathering in a big valley. The ministers were wearing exquisite clothes and precious ornaments. Then they brought an elephant holding a 'vase of long life' by its trunk and made it search from someone among the crowd. The elephant waved its trunk and pushed aside all the ministers and the subjects and came running towards the king and the poor couple's son. Then the elephant placed the vase on the king's head. As soon as the elephant placed the vase, the ministers and the subjects surrounded them and played music. The king was escorted somewhere, but the poor couple's son did not know where. He was left there, confused. Moreover, he could not find a way to return home. Therefore, he rented a room in the house of a mother and a daughter. He was very thirsty and asked for some wine. The mother and the daughter asked, "How would you like to pay?" He replied, "I will pay in gold." They served all their wine to him. That night, he got drunk and slept as if he was dead. At about midnight, the wine took its effect and he vomited up gold. The old mother and the daughter took a lamp and looked around. They found all of his vomit was gold. To get more gold, they forced butter down into his mouth, hoping that he will vomit more gold. After a while, he vomited a snake. They thought the snake must be the reason for his gold vomit. Therefore, the mother washed the snake and made her daughter swallow it. As she coughed out, her vomit turned into gold. When he woke up, he coughed to pay for the wine, but nothing came out. He said to the old mother, "You can take all my gold for your wine, but would you care to return the snake, please?" The old mother shouted, "Where did this beggar come from? With nothing to pay for your food and wine, do you dare charge me for burglary?" Then she began to hit him hard. He lamented, "Oh! Once I had the luck to spend time with a king. Now I have become unhappy and I can not vomit gold." He thought it would be shameful to return home, so he decided to leave for the upper valley and commit suicide.

As the poor couple's son walked on, he saw three boys fighting over a bag, shoes and a hat. He went near them, and asked, "Why are you boys fighting?" They replied, "We are fighting for the bag, shoes and the hat. These magical shoes take you wherever you desire. The hat, if worn, makes you invisible. The bag can provide as much meat and butter as you wish." He said, "You should run a race. I will give the first one the bag, the second one will get the hat and the third one will get the shoes." The children said, "How good to find a good man like you," and then they left to run the race. He looked like he was ready to give each item back, he carried the bag on his back and he held the shoes in his hand, but then he quickly put on the hat. The three boys started their race, but as they came back and reached the end of the race, they could no not see him. The boys blamed each other and then they went away.

Then the poor couple's son climbed a rock and saw a huge tree nearby. As he remained under that tree, he saw a three-

headed demon coming. He put the hat on his head and sat there. The demon could not see him. Then the demon plucked a blue flower, which changed him into an old monkey and then climbed up the tree. The next morning, when the sun rose, the monkey came down. He plucked a yellow flower and turned into a demon. The poor couple's son also plucked a blue and a yellow flower, wore the shoes and wished, "Take me to where the wicked mother and the daughter are." Fantastically he was already there. Then he called out for the old mother and daughter. As the daughter came out, he left for her to see and to pick up the blue flower. As the daughter picked up the blue flower, she changed into a horrible looking old female monkey. As he had his hat on, he was invisible to her. Then when she went inside and said, "Mother, no one is at the door." The old mother was frightened to see her daughter changed into a monkey. She thought that it was the work of the elderly couple's son. She searched all around, but could not find him.

Then the poor couple's son showed himself at their door with the shoes hanging from his waist and the hat folded securely in his bag. As the old mother saw him, she bowed down in front of him and requested him to, "Please, take all your gold and take back the snake too." He said, "As the saying goes, 'answer comes not when you ask, but when you watch and wait,' now get my gold and the snake." The old mother and her daughter, who still looked like a monkey, both bowed down to him. Being a kind man, he said, "Just give me my snake. I will change you back to a human." Then they returned to the house and made the daughter vomit up the snake. He washed the snake and swallowed it. He took the daughter into a room. He asked her, "What does your mother want from me?" The daughter said, "What a pity. I am in a sorry shape. My mother wants me to have a real human face." Then he gave her the yellow flower. In an instant, she transformed from a monkey back into a girl. Both the old mother and the daughter were very happy. They brought all the gold and again bowed down repeatedly to him. He kindly gave them back the gold.

The poor couple's son then put on his magical shoes, carried the bag on his back, put on the hat and wished, "May I see the king." Suddenly, he arrived at the place where the king was. Initially frightened, the king slowly recognized him and they embraced. He offered the bag that gave meat and butter. Together they rode on an elephant, accompanied by many ministers and subjects, they returned to the former kingdom. There, the fortunate son of the elderly couple was enthroned as the king and both had kingdoms to rule. While the kingdom on this side treasured a great golden tortoise, the kingdom on the other side had the bag that gave meat and butter. Both kingdoms became very prosperous and they both ruled in accordance with the Dharma. Their subjects and attendants too lived happy lives.

Then Prince Gautamiputra remarked, "How fortunate was that man!" The corpse said, "Oh prince! At last, you spoke to the corpse." The Siddhivad corpse slapped the prince three times and swiftly flew away.

Here ends the thirty-second Siddhivad corpse story, The Fortunate Man.

33 A Brother and a Sister

Prince Gautamiputra thought, "I have been at fault for being distracted and speaking too much. I cannot go back to master Nāgārjuna without the Siddhivad corpse." Once again, the prince returned to Sītavana cemetery and stood at the foot of the tree. The prince grabbed and kicked the corpse as the corpse cried out, "Aah! Ooh!" Again, the prince put the corpse into the bag, tied it with a rope and carried it on his back. After seven steps, the Siddhivad corpse said, "Prince, tell me a story. This will make our way virtually shorter." The prince thought, "I know what this corpse is up to." Then the corpse said, "There is no way I could get to hear a story from your mouth. Anyway, I will tell you a short story. Just listen."

The Siddhivad corpse then narrated the following story:

Once upon a time, there was a brother and a sister whose parents had died many years ago; they were orphans. In the upper part of the valley, there were two demons named, Zachen and Zachung.

The young girl tended to their flock of sheep and one day, with the hope of finding good pasture, took her flock up the valley. That day, a boy from the other side of the pass came to graze his flock of sheep in the same pasture as the girl. When he saw her, the boy proposed to her saying, "Would you marry me?" The girl shyly replied, "Yes." Then he asked, "We must seek your brother's permission for our marriage." She objected, "No. You do not need to ask my brother. Even if my brother was dead, I would still live with you." The boy said, "There are two demons, Zachen and Zachung, in the upper valley. This evening, just pretend to be sick. I think that your brother is kind and will ask you what would cure your sickness. Tell him that there is a remedy, but it is something that is impossible for him to accomplish. He will insist that he would do anything to rid you of your sickness.

In that case, tell him that in the upper valley live two demons, Zachen and Zachung. Say to him, 'If you could get some garlic from their garden, it would cure me. Brother, could you do that?' He would promise to do anything for you. Then, as he enters the demons' garden to pick the garlic, the enraged demons will eat him. Also, tell your brother, that you and he will still live together."

Then the younger sister returned home. There she placed some red ink on the right side of her mouth and some red ink on the left side of her face and cried, "Ooh! Ouch! What a pain!" The brother asked, "What do you think will help cure this?" The younger sister said, "While I was grazing my flock, the forest spirits harmed me. There is a remedy for this sickness, but you can't do it." Then he said, "Our parents are not with us. If there is anything I could do to alleviate your pain, I will do it." Then she said, "In the upper valley, there is garlic growing in the garden of a demon called, Zachen. If you could bring me some of that garlic, it will surely cure my illness. But can you really do that?" He said, "If it truly cures, then I can do it."

Then the brother rode on a fine horse, took a dog with him and left for the upper valley. He cut garlic plants from the Zachen's garden. The demon Zachen saw him and was shocked as nobody dared take garlic from his garden. So, Zachen shouted, "Beggar, how dare you!" The girl's brother rolled up his sleeves and dashed towards Zachen. The clever horse was startled as soon as he saw this. The dog grabbed Zachen's feet in his mouth, as the brother hit a heavy stone on Zachen's legs. As Zachen collapsed, he cried, "Please don't kill me. I will do whatever you want. If you ask me to hit, I will even hit my own father's head. If you ask me to eat, I will even eat his liver. If you ask me to go, I will even go to hell." He swore these things to the brother to spare him, so the brother did not kill Zachen. Then the brother returned home with lots of garlic, which he gave to his sister.

The next day, the sister pretended to be well and was cured. She went to herd her sheep and again met the boy. He asked, "Is your brother dead?" She replied, "He didn't die, instead he collected a lot of garlic plants and returned home safe. He made

Zachen his servant." The boy said, "Do you think that your brother is great? Now, let him collect garlic from demon Zachung's garden. Pretend you have intense pain in the groin and say, 'I'll die if you don't bring me garlic from the demon Zachung's garden." She again pretended to be sick and her brother insisted on finding a cure for his sister's pain. Once again, he rode his horse, took the dog and this time, also took his servant Zachen and left for Zachung's garden.

After the brother had collected a bagful of garlic, Zachung saw Zachen. Zachung rolled up his sleeves and shouted at him, "You beggar. How dare you bring a man into my garden, where no man ever trespassed." Demon Zachung slapped Zachen three times and rushed towards the girl's brother. But the brother rode his horse and caught Zachung by his neck. Zachen was angry and blocked Zachung's way. The dog pulled at Zachung's belly, whereby he collapsed. Zachung then pleaded, "Please, don't kill me. I'll do what you want. If you ask me to hit, I will even hit my father's head. If you ask me to eat, I will even eat my mother's liver. I'll do whatever you ask me to do. If you ask me to go, I can even go to hell." He swore his allegiance several times. The brother left to return home, taking Zachung and with Zachen following them carrying a load of garlic. When they reached home, he gave a lot more garlic to his sister.

The next day, the sister climbed the pass with her sheep and met the boy. The boy asked, "Did you kill your brother?" She replied, "My brother brought home a lot of garlic and brought home the subdued demon Zachung as well." The boy said, "Do you still think that your brother is great? Now return home, lie in your bed and pretend you are twisting in pain. When your brother asks what could he do, you must tell him that you had taken too much garlic. That you now have a stomachache and have lost your appetite. Tell him that there is a remedy, but you don't want to put him into any more trouble. If your brother says, 'I will do whatever I can,' tell him to collect salt from the ocean far away. I am sure he will die on this voyage." The sister did as she was instructed. She pretended to be sick and said, "Only sea salt can

cure me." The brother said, "If it can cure you, I will brave all the hardships."

The bother saddled up the horse, followed by the two demons and his two dogs and he left for the sea. Then, as he arrived at the shore, he saw that sea salt can be gathered only from the center of the ocean. He attached a long rope to his waist and entered the ocean with a bag, while Zachen held the other end of the rope on the shore. The brother said, "When I pull the rope, it means the bag is full of salt and you should pull and bring the bag of salt to the shore." After a while, when Zachen pulled the rope, there was nothing on the other end. Zachen said, "There is nothing we could do. He asked the dogs and the horse to drink water from the ocean. Zachung, you drink and drain all the sea water." The dogs and the horse drank a lot, but the water level remained the same. Then as Zachung took some gulps, the water level decreased slightly. He set his teeth and poured the seawater beyond the pass. It created a heavy flood in the valley. Then Zachen drank a lot of water and the water finally drained out. Zachen saw ground salt settled as sand at the center and quickly filled the bag with salt. Zachen searched for the brother's bones, but could not find any. As Zachen drank the remaining water and poured it out, he found some bones. Then as Zachung drank the rest, more bones were recovered. Zachen said to Zachung, "We are bound by a pledge with our master. You should quickly go to my house now. At my house, there is a small vase of nectar given to me by my mother. I knew it would come to use one day. I hid it on a shelf above the columns. Bring it here." Zachung went to his house. He took the small vase off the shelf, slipped it in his pocket and ate some food. He returned just before dark. However, Zachen thought that Zachung failed to return, so Zachen slept there on the beach.

The next morning, Zachung came by and applied the nectar on the brother's skeleton and restored him back to life. When Zachung applied more nectar on the surface, both flesh and blood were restored. Then Zachung dropped a pill with the nectar into the mouth to restore more flesh. He used another pill to restore his skin and a yet another pill to retrieve his consciousness. At that time, Zachen woke up. Then, they loaded the sea salt and the brother returned home with his demons, attendants and the dogs. He let his sister take the sea salt. She faked instant recovery.

The next day, the sister drove the flock of sheep to the pass and met the boy again. The boy asked, "Is your brother dead." She replied, "No, he is not. He brought sea salt and forced me to take it." He said, "Now, I think your brother is indeed great." The sister said, "Unless my brother dies, we cannot be husband and wife. Is there any remedy?" He said, "Now there is no way. If I begged him for your hand in marriage, he won't agree." She began to cry and tears rolled down her cheeks. Then he asked, "Don't cry. Do you think you can kill your brother?" She replied, "Yes, I can kill him." Then he explained, "Tonight, tell your brother that he must be very tired and serve him a lot of wine. Keep a log under his pillow and then around midnight, throw a big stone on his head to kill him. The two demons must not know anything about this. Then flee immediately on the horse." The girl then returned home with the flock of sheep.

As she was told, she said to her brother, "You must be very tired. I have set the bed for you. Sleep well." She prepared the bed and hid a log under the pillow, after that she served a lot of wine to him. At midnight, she got up without disturbing the demons. Lifting a big stone, she moved towards her brother's pillow. The brother, having felt uncomfortable with the usual hardness of his pillow, had placed it on the other end of the bed. The sister dropped the big stone where his pillow used to be. The brother suddenly woke up and shouted, "Who is there? Zachen and Zachung come to me!" Zachen and Zachung came with a lamp. They looked everywhere, but they saw no one. The girl had run away, saddled the horse and was about to flee. Zachen said, "It is this witch! She tried to harm you another time before. Don't let her flee." He caught the girl and swallowed her. When the brother cried out, "Do not do anything to her." Zachen said, "I have already swallowed her." The brother said, "You did a bad thing for all the good things I did for you. What bad things had my sister done? It's a pity, I am suffering for this regrettable act." The demon Zachen said, "Whatever we do, be it good or bad, is meant for your good. I have a potion for this, but I won't give it to you." The brother said, "It's just me and my sister in this family. Despite all her harm, I still can't be separated from her. It is a pity." He dedicated all his wealth for her merits and he released the demons, Zachen and Zachung.

Then the brother rode his horse, took the two dogs and left for a distant place to find some relief from his grief. He stopped near a lake and let his horse graze on the rich pasture. There he found a comb, a shell rosary and a mirror. The horse said, "Take them, you never know when you might need them." With those things, he sat at the edge of the lake. After a while, the lake began to rise. The horse cried out, "Saddle your horse quickly, take the dogs and flee." He saddled the horse, took the two dogs and fled. He saw a she-wolf as big as a hill rise up from the middle of the lake and it chased him. When it was very close, the horse said, "Make a wish and throw the comb." He threw the comb and it turned into a forest. As the wolf moved around the forest, it lost its way, the brother was able to escape.

Once again, when the brother encountered the she-wolf, the horse cried, "Say your prayers and fling the shell rosary at her." As he threw the shell rosary, a snow mountain as white as a conch shell filled the land, whereby the brother escaped from the wolf.

Later, as the she-wolf chased them again, the horse shouted, "Pray and throw the mirror." He prayed, "May a lake appear the same as this mirror, with fire from all sides and make me free on this side. May no one walk around it or across the lake, nor swim in it." Everything he prayed for miraculously appeared. From the other shore of the lake, the she-wolf cried, "Beggar, you owe me your life and your previous birth. It is with the help of the beggars Zachen and Zachung and your horse, that you are safe and alive." Then the she-wolf returned to the lake. In a previous life, the brother had taken his sister's life. To revenge her death, that sister was born in the form of a she-wolf. This is how he owed a life to her.

Then the brother arrived at a vast empty place. The horse knew that he was going to die soon and said, "Brother, I am now going to die. You should not cry when I die. Take off my skin and spread it on the ground, keep the head at the center and place the heart in the mouth. Take out all the teeth and scatter them over the meadow. Place the two kidneys near the head, spread the stomach on the ground and throw the intestines around the skin. Take the lungs to a high area, cut the liver into pieces and place the pieces around the lung. Take off the hair and scatter it in the hills. Place the bile near the head. Remember, do not cry, if you cry, it will be cold." Then the horse died.

The brother was very sad and cried over the loss of his horse, which had saved his life from the spell of his sister through the power of her previous Karma. Then there was heavy rain and snowfall. The brother suddenly stopped crying and there was warm sunshine. He did as the horse had instructed. He was tired and slept the whole day. At about midday, a boy called out, "Wake up! Don't sleep like this." As the boy shook his head, he woke up. He thought, "My sister had been a witch and was after my life and my horse has died. Now who could it be?" He looked and saw a handsome boy adorned with various ornaments. The boy said, "Wake up. I was the horse, who had to repay your kindness from previous lives."

Then the brother got up and there was a girl there who invited him into a magnificent palace. It was an excellent nine-storey palace standing above a massive horse head. The horse's heart that had been placed inside the horse's mouth had turned into this beautiful girl. Two nice horses appeared from the two kidneys. The intestines surrounding the skin had now become a strong fence. The lungs scattered around became wise ministers and the hair had transformed into a rich forest. The stomach spread on the ground became nice pastures and the teeth scattered around became fine snow mountains, which gave water to the entire valley. What resulted from dividing the liver into a left side and a right side, became two big rocky mountains that surrounded the area. Between the mountains was a road. The two parts of the

liver also became three children. Those three children were like gods and would dedicate their lives to practicing the Dharma, day and night.

Then Prince Gautamiputra remarked, "The brother loved his sister very much, but the sister was bent upon taking her brother's life. It was the kind horse that actually saved his life." The corpse slapped the prince three times and said, "You finally said something." The Siddhivad corpse swiftly flew away.

Here ends the thirty-third Siddhivad corpse story, A Brother and a Sister.

34 The Unmarried Weaver

Once again, Prince Gautamiputra had barely taken seven steps from the cemetery and the Siddhivad corpse said, "Oh prince, what happened?" The prince knew the corpse was expecting a reply and he remained silent. The corpse said, "This unfortunate prince will never talk. Listen, I will tell you a story."

The Siddhivad corpse then narrated the following story:

Once upon a time, there was a great king in a kingdom where there lived a man-eating tiger in the upper part of the valley. Each year, the king sent three of his subjects as food for the tiger. An unmarried weaver lived in the upper part of the valley and on the opposite side there lived a mother with her two sons. Although they lived happily together, one of the sons was a foster child.

One day, it was the mother and her two sons whose turn it was to go as food for the man-eating tiger. The tiger came to their house and entered the gate, but before eating them, he thought, "I can eat them anytime. Why not first eavesdrop to see what they are talking about?" The mother and the sons were discussing what would happen to their property and their wealth after their death. They sat around a huge fire and baked bread stuffed with meat and butter, but they baked plain bread for the foster son. When the fat began to come out from the bread with meat, it made the foster son unhappy, as his was the plain, dry bread. Feeling deeply upset, he thought, "Whatever had happened in the past, we are all going to die tonight. Now she will not have any of her wealth, her real son is also upset about this too." The mother said, "How sad that we will soon be eaten by the tiger." The stepson said, "Mother, don't be upset, there is nothing to be sad about. Many of the subjects in the kingdom suffered the same fate. There are more serious things to feel sad about." The stepmother said, "What more do we have to worry about, for we shall be eaten by the tiger tonight." The stepson replied, "The tiger has reasons to be evil. However, there is an animal called Śarabha[1] which is more ferocious than the tiger that will come to eat us tonight. Even more frightening than Śarabha is Dale Nokya."[2] The tiger thought, "If those two ferocious animals come here, I'll be helpless. So, maybe I will just eat their old spotted bull in the courtyard instead." So, he ate the old spotted bull and slept there.

The unmarried weaver in the upper part of the valley thought, "The moon has risen and waxed fully. The man-eating tiger must have eaten those people at midnight by now. I should go and steal their old bull." He took off his clothes, picked up an ax in his right hand and a noose in his left hand. Then stealthily, he walked towards the house of the mother and her sons. It was midnight of the full moon, there was no noise from anybody or from the dogs. The tiger slept on the window sill of the dimly lit compound. Mistaking the tiger for the bull, he tied a rope around its neck. The tiger thinking it could be Śarabha sprang up and was standing on his legs. The man had caught a man-eating tiger. He was not frightened and he got on the tiger's back and rode him holding on to the ears. They left the area and traveled over eighteen passes and valleys.

When the sun rose, they approached a big sandalwood tree that had a Garuḍa's nest in it. A few nights ago, on the eve of the full moon, some Garuḍa chicks hatched in the nest. At the base of that tree was a big poisonous snake, which was ready to climb up the tree and eat the chicks. The unmarried weaver threw his rope towards the tree at what he thought was a brace, but the noose caught the snake by its tail. The snake turned around and attacked the middle of the tiger's body. The tiger tore the snake apart and the two died.

Many herders from the upper valley saw that man riding the tiger and they saw him catching the poisonous snake with a rope. They also saw the two animals fight and finally kill each other. Then the herders ran to the palace and reported that incident to

the king. When the king sent his senior ministers there, they found him skinning the tiger. One of the ministers asked, "Are you well? Our great king has invited you to come to the palace." He went to the palace with the tiger skin wrapped around his body. The king gave his princess to him as his wife and named him 'Tiger-riding and snake noose-holding son-in-law.'[3]

Sometime later, a woman running a beer bar invited him to her bar. After getting very drunk, the weaver returned to his wife and told her, "I want to sleep, prepare my bed." As she prepared the bed, he crept into the bed sheets and proudly said, "I was a bachelor from the upper valley. I went to steal the bull that belonged to a mother and her sons. I mistook the tiger for the bull, but I was filled with joy as I rode on it. The tiger took me across many passes and valleys. Again mistaking a poisonous snake for a branch, I threw a rope and it caught the snake by its tail. The snake fell down and attacked the tiger. The tiger could not bear the pain and retaliated. Finally, both the animals died. Then while I was skinning the tiger, the king's ministers invited me to the palace. As I appeared before the king, he gave your hand to me for marriage. I was actually just an unmarried weaver from the upper valley. I am not sure, if I am worthy to be your husband. Maybe, it's better to survive on a staple diet and live in the upper valley." The princess became angry and went to the king. There she wept bitterly and complained, "I am your only daughter and I could have married a great man. From what I heard from my husband, he seemed to be just a weaver from the upper valley and that's unacceptable to me." The king said, "Don't be sad, let me closely examine your husband." The king summoned his wise ministers and said, "In the upper region of our kingdom, there is a man-eating wolf and each year, we sacrifice a person as food to this creature. Ask my son-in-law to subdue this wolf. Give him whatever weapons he may need."

A wise minister took a jar of wine with him and went into the small house of the king's son-in-law. While serving the wine, the wise minister asked, "Tell me, what would you need to quash a man-eating wolf, to whom we sacrifice a man each year?" The weaver thought, "I am just a weaver and all I have is my only work tool, a loom. What could make a good weapon?" So he kept staring at the beams in the house, while murmuring something. He said, "Wings wide like a Garuḍa's and a beam as long as a poisonous snake." The minister said, "Yes, I get it." The weaver could not say anything else, he was too terrified.

The minister went back to the king and said, "Your son-in-law needs a bow as big as the beam in a house and an arrow as big as a pillar." The king hired people to cut a tall willow tree from the king's garden to make the bow. They twisted many hides to make the bowstrings. A straight willow made the arrow. They employed a blacksmith to sharpen the arrow point. Then they carried the bow and the arrow to the weaver's place and gave it to him.

The weaver went to the wolf's den and thought, "The wolf must be inside this den. If he sees me, he might kill me." So, he slept outside, near the den. The wolf was not in the den, he was away hunting. When the wolf returned, he saw the huge bow and began nibbling at the bowstring. As the bowstring snapped, it hit the wolf's nose and killed him. As the weaver decided to leave thinking that the wolf really was not inside the den, he saw the dead wolf. He went to the wolf, dragged him around, cut a hole through his ribs and thrust the arrow inside his body. Then he went to the king and said, "I have killed the man eating monstrous wolf. I need someone to bring it here." The king sent a minister with many people to bring back the wolf's dead body. They skinned the wolf, took the bow and arrow and brought it all back to the king. The king summoned the princess and said, "You told me that he is an unmarried weaver from the upper valley, but now look at this wolf skin. He must be a manifestation of the mighty Masang."[4] The princess was pleased and they lived together again.

As time passed, the king held a grand feast and again, the weaver got very drunk. He said to his wife, "I was an unmarried weaver from the upper valley. While asleep near the den, the wolf, out of curiosity, chewed on my bowstring. The bowstring snapped and killed the wolf. So, I am now the husband of a princess. Before I was just an unmarried weaver from the upper valley. I can survive on whatever falls into my hand." The princess reported this to the king and said, "Being your only daughter, how could you give me to such a man?" The king said, "Princess, he is a manifestation of the mighty Masang. He is the right husband for you. We can check if he was truly an unmarried weaver or not." Then the king said, "Our kingdom is facing the danger of an enemy invasion. Let my son-in-law command an army to defend our kingdom. Wise minister, go and ask what he would need for weapons."

The wise minister took a jar of wine and served it to the king's son-in-law in a garden. Then the minister asked, "Invaders are advancing and they will soon attack our kingdom. You have to command our forces and defend us. Please, tell me what weapons you would need for this purpose." The weaver again wondered, "I am only a weaver and a loom is my only tool. What weapons should I ask?" There in the garden, he saw garlic plants with large ripe garlic bulbs[5] ready to be picked. Absentmindedly, he uttered, "White root and spicy too. Triple pronged like a trident and a strong armed force." The wise minister said, "Yes, I got it." He reported this to the king, "Oh king, your son-in-law needs a swift striped stallion for his mount, a trident and a strong force too. Then he will fight back the enemy force, the day after tomorrow."

As the day arrived, the weaver mounted a swift striped horse and wore strong armor. Fastening the trident tightly on the horse, he led the armed force to fight the enemy. The enemy soldiers thought that he must be the brave son-in-law of the king, who they heard was one who rides tigers. Then, as the enemy force attacked from the front, they suffered counter attacks from all their sides. Fighting for sometime, the striped horse was disturbed and ran among the enemy force. Mindlessly, the weaver shouted, "Angatrukjed!" The weaver's army thought the weaver wanted them to retreat. However, the weaver shouted, "Shout like me and run and let the horse run free." He could not control the horse, which ran aimlessly around the battleground. As the trident

tied on the horse hit many soldiers, they all died. The enemy soldiers thought that he was a brave man and thus they immediately retreated.

Finally, the weaver heading the royal soldiers in battle, returned victorious. When the soldiers reached the palace, the king said to the princess, "Do you still think he is a bachelor weaver of the upper valley? What could only be true about him is that only a woman can overcome him, just like a stallion for whom only a mare would dare frolic." The princess was ecstatic. The king and the ministers were happy and they too were convinced.

As the king had no son, he made the weaver his successor and the king lived a reclusive life. The weaver and the princess gave birth to three sons and two daughters. The kingdom thrived and had more happiness, wealth and prosperity.

As the corpse concluded his story, Prince Gautamiputra unmindfully said, "The stepson was not as lucky as the unmarried weaver." The corpse jeered, "Oh prince, you finally spoke to this corpse. Now I will fly away." The Siddhivad corpse slapped him three times and escaped.

Prince Gautamiputra recounted how his teacher Nāgārjuna severely criticized his behavior in the past. Thus the prince returned to the same cemetery and to the tree where the Siddhivad corpse was in. He hit the corpse with a club, the corpse cried, "Aaah! Laa!" Then he kicked the corpse, making the corpse cry out, "Oooh! Loo!"

Here ends the thirty-fourth Siddhivad corpse story, The Unmarried Weaver.

---

1. Tib. Su ru kha sbob (Skt. Śarabha).
2. Tib. Gdah le sno skya.
3. Tib. Tsha no ngom gyis stag shon zer phyag na sbrul shags mnams pa, meaning son-in-law who rides a tiger and holds a snake noose in hand.
4. Tib. Ma sang, also spelt Ma bzan, is considered a class of being inhabiting the Tibetan plateau, long before the human life began.
5. Tib. Sor gang, literally full finger, means a finger wide, approximately measuring 2 cm.